A BOY FROM
THE STREETS

MARIA GIBBS

Copyright

I would like to thank everyone who has inspired or supported me in my writing throughout the years. I would also like to thank you the reader for purchasing a copy. I hope you enjoy reading it.

Dedication

I'd like to dedicate this book to an amazing young man who I am proud to call my son. Mark has gone through more than his fair share of hardships in life. Despite enjoying a good moan, daily, Mark is happy, bright and extremely caring. Love you, my darling.

Table of Contents

Also by this Author

Coming Soon

Prologue (12th September 1981)

Leandro

"Leandro, you and Carolina must leave now."

"Carolina is in labour. She cannot be moved."

"As soon as she has birthed the baby, you will both leave."

"The baby will be too young to be moved so soon."

"You will leave it behind. It will be cared for."

"We cannot countenance such an action."

"You have no choice."

"There is always a choice."

"Alright, Leandro, then your choice is this: take your wife and leave the child in my care, or stay, and you will all die."

The Professor's eyebrows drew together, the quivering dark hairs touching before his face relaxed and they returned to their normal resting place. "Promise me you will take care of my child until I can come back."

"You have my solemn promise, Leandro. I will care for your child until you can return with Carolina. The baby will, after all, be my niece or nephew."

Warm air brushed against his skin, and yet, Leandro still shivered. Trusting his brother was not easy, for theirs had never been a close relationship, but blood ties were strong.

The Professor slipped away and met with his colleague. "I must leave my child behind, Daniel."

"Who will care for the child?"

"Paolo."

Daniel's quick intake of breath coupled with his expression showed his distaste.

"I know, my friend, but I can trust my brother with this."

"As you please, Leandro. May God go with you and Carolina."

"What will you do?"

"I cannot leave my beloved Rio, so I shall take to the streets. I will live on the fringes of society, unnoticed and unimportant."

"But you are important, my friend, we both are. We have stumbled on the biggest—"

"Shush, you mustn't say anything else." Daniel looked around but the only witness to their conversation was the bright-coloured mural decorating the side of the building. An image of a boy stared down at them with an expression that told of the misery he had endured.

"You're right. God go with you, Daniel Cortez."

Both men clasped the other in a bear hug, a symbol of their solidarity. Neither was ashamed of the tear that welled in their eyes, and neither turned back to watch the other walk away.

Carolina

Carolina and Leandro held one baby each. Both were struck dumb momentarily by the perfection of their two babies when only one had been expected. Fingers and toes so delicate, and little rosebud lips which split as mewling cries escaped them in unison. Tears streamed from Carolina's eyes, but she was careful not to allow herself to lose control and disturb the babies, she would save that for later. She didn't want their memory of her, their mother, to be tainted when they were reunited. Her fingertips brushed against the downy texture of her baby's skin, causing another wave of love and fear to mix and form a nauseous knot in her stomach.

"I can't." She whimpered.

"We must, my darling. For their sakes, not ours."

The nurse in the starched white apron took charge by removing the baby from Carolina, placing him in swaddling, and then into a cot that was much too big for him now, but into which he would grow. Then she went to take his twin from his father. Carolina interrupted her, and took the child from her husband's arms so she could hold him to her breast for one last time. Showering love on him as she had his brother, she touched his skin and placed a kiss on his forehead. With a strength she did not feel in her trembling arms, Carolina proffered the bundle to the nurse, who swaddled him and then placed him so he was side-by-side with his twin, their heads touching.

Carolina took one last look at her babies, drinking in the sight of them, burning them on her memory for all-time, and inhaling the sweet smell before stumbling away. Her legs refused to work, buckling beneath her. She would have fallen had Leandro not wrapped his arms around her and led her away. Her control left her and she sought to return to the twins, to shelter them and love them. When this was not possible, she howled, like a wolf purportedly does to the moon.

It was a few minutes later that the sound of two gunshots rang out, echoing in the silence of the hospital grounds. No one stopped what they were doing;

everyone continued going about their business as though the sounds were those of the distant fireworks which lit up the night sky at Carnival.

Two figures skulking in the shadows stepped out and ran to the prone figures on the floor.

The Orphanage Brasil
(19th September 1981)

Christina

"Fernando, we must take them both, we cannot separate twins."

"Christina, you're too soft, we can't bring up two children. You're not strong enough to cope with the needs of twins. Your constitution is weak. It would be unfair to all of us."

"I know my health is delicate, Fernando, and I will always regret that I can't carry your baby to term inside me, but I know I can love and care for these twins. We can afford to hire help…" She trailed off when she saw the determined jut of his chin, the expression that brooked no further argument. Christina decided to try one last tug at his conscience anyway. "If we leave one behind, he might end up on the streets, an urchin living in squalor and fighting to survive… if he even makes it past babyhood."

"Christina, your abundance of love does you credit, but I have no doubts the other boy will be adopted also. The only thing left to do now is to choose which one you would like?"

Christina's heart sank as she looked at the two bundles in front of her. He was asking her to choose one, like picking out a pair of shoes from the rows on display in a shop. One stirred and let out a howl, disturbing his twin. It was almost as though he were alert to the inherent danger in this situation and was warning his brother.

Christina reached out a hand to each of them, touching their delicate tiny fingers and marvelling at how small, how fragile they were. Both lay quietly now, staring up at her with eyes as yet unable to focus. The boy who had been woken by his brother curled his tiny digits around her finger. In that moment she knew. He was asking her for help. The other twin would have the strength and tenacity to face whatever life threw at him. Christina couldn't think about that, now that the decision was made. There was no hope of changing Fernando's mind.

Without a further glance to the brother, she scooped up her new baby, cradling his floppy head and bringing him close to her chest so that he could feel her heart beat and know he was safe. She started to walk away with Fernando's supportive hand between her shoulder blades. The baby in her arms let out a whimpering cry, and his twin, who still lay in the cot, responded with a heart-breaking howl which tore at her heartstrings and caused Christina to pause her flight. Fernando's hand applied gentle pressure while she lifted one leaden foot in front of the other. A silent tear fell from her face onto the baby in her arms. She muttered a quick prayer for his twin.

"All that's left now is to fill in the paperwork and the boy is ours." Fernando's handsome face broke into a smile. He reached out and touched the silent baby in his wife's arms.

"You are to be our son," he crooned. "We must think of a fitting name to honour your new status in the Sanchez family."

"Jose, after your father." Christina dimpled as Fernando rewarded her with a winning smile then pulled her and their new baby into his arms before placing a gentle kiss on her lips.

Chapter One

Twelve years Later – Brasil

Jose

The plane's wheels touched the runway, the force of the reverse thrust impelling me forward while the seatbelt pushed into my abdomen. I realized that I was gripping my book whose pages I'd pressed together on descent, after inserting the bookmark between the sheets, so that I could savour the new experience. The plane had glided low over the sea, providing me with a view of the azure waters sparkling an invitation below. I grinned at the thought of all these new thrills associated with flying; I had especially loved the sensation of taking off and landing. If I closed my eyes, I could almost believe I was soaring like a bird over the majestic mountains which looked superimposed on the skyline. Images conjured up and tumbled around inside my head of adventures that could be had; although the sum of my adventures lay in the pages of the books I devoured. Father flew regularly for business, but this was the first time that he'd taken *Mamãe* and me along with him.

I felt his speculative gaze on me, knowing I was a disappointment to him. Intelligent but not sporty, my health was less than robust. He never said a word of criticism, but I knew well the look he gave me when he thought I wasn't looking. I knew he wondered how he could have fathered me. I'd once overheard him berate *Mamãe* for her "choice," though I'd not known what he'd meant by that. I had pondered his words for a few days but hadn't dared broach the subject knowing that he would become angry, and *Mamãe* would be sad. Since I'd inherited her weak constitution, perhaps Father felt that she had trained me to be ill, that it was her doing. Maybe that was what he'd meant. He was right that she mollycoddled me, but when I felt ill, the comfort of my *mamãe's* arms were a welcome respite.

"Welcome home, Jose." *Mamãe* squeezed my arm, her excitement was infectious.

"*Mamãe*, England is my home. I've never been to Brasil before."

"You were here as a *bebê*."

I intercepted a look Father shot at *Mamãe*; her response was a placatory smile.

"You'll have a chance to practise your Portuguese while you are here, Jose." She was trying to distract me.

I often wondered what had brought them together. *Mamãe* loved Father, it was clear, yet she seemed to be reserved in the way she was with him. Loving and gentle with a fantastic sense of humour, she often enjoyed the ridiculous—but I never saw her like that when Father was around. She held back in front of him, and seemed as though she were walking a continual tight-rope. Despite all that, she adored him. I could understand her attitude, though, because I, too, hid my true self from him. My father thought of me as a bumbling geek.

I knew, too, that Father loved *Mamãe*, because despite his harsh demeanour, I also saw the soft, loving glances he threw in her direction when he believed himself to be unobserved. Similar to when he threw me ones of disgust. I'd become good at blending into the shadows, and learned to observe many things.

"Come on, Jose, we don't want to be on this airplane all day." Father snapped.

Pedro

My stomach hurt so much I feared that I was dying. *If I don't get some food soon, I probably will.* Starvation was a horrible thing. I thought about the emaciated body of my old friend, Jonny. It wasn't his real name, just as Pedro wasn't mine. We were *pivetinho*, we weren't given names, didn't have identities. We couldn't cease to exist because we didn't exist in the first place. The *polícia* could come by and do another shooting, and no one except the other vagabonds would know of our demise. A lump formed in my throat and a tear clouded my vision thinking about Jonny. I wiped the evidence of my wet eyes away. It didn't pay to show weakness on the street. Weakness was exploited. You had to be tough.

I couldn't allow myself to dwell on Jonny's death, and yet, I couldn't stop. I'd tried to give him a bigger share of the meagre portions of food I scraped from the bins, begged, or stole. His body was too weak in the end to go out himself, his bones jutting through the film of his skin. My mind kept straying to the night nearly six months before, when Jonny and I lay huddled together for warmth. The heat of the day had gone, leaving a chill in its place. DC threw himself down beside us.

"*Olá,* boys, have you made any money today?"

"No, DC," I answered for both of us. "Jonny has been bad today."

Despite the darkness of the shadows where he sat, I knew DC was worried. DC was our surrogate *pai*. A man of indeterminable age, he had rescued us both from the gutter, and certain death. A long, straggly beard covered the lower half of his face which was framed by the long length of greasy black hair he allowed to cover himself. DC always walked with his head down and his back stooped, but he never missed a thing that happened. Jonny and I had both been abandoned by the orphanage when we'd reached the grand old age of one year. No one had taken us, and by then, no one would. Childless couples came to adopt but they wanted babies, not one-year-olds who they couldn't pass off as their own. The orphanage wasn't a charitable organisation. They creamed a healthy profit from selling babies to desperate couples. When a child didn't sell, they had no use for them. Jonny and I, and a bunch of other kids, were abandoned in an *aléia* a few blocks from the orphanage. That's where DC found us one night, and he took us in.

DC taught us to pick pockets, and we all shared what we'd managed to procure that day. But times were hard, too many of us were living the street life, and we couldn't always get a touch. Invariably, we could go days without food. He clothed us; to be precise, he took the rags from dead street urchins, if they were in a reasonable condition, for us. There was a real market in these rags, so we felt like kings in our tattered finery. Tattered finery–an oxymoron. The other thing DC gave us was an education. DC had once, if it were to be believed, been quite a hotshot lawyer. He'd owned his own house and had earned a weekly wage that would feed and clothe every *pivetinho* in royal style for a year. Something had happened, though; and he never told us what.

Some of the boys said his wife had cheated on him, so in a rage, he had killed her. After that, he disappeared into the anonymity of the streets because he couldn't bear to flee his beloved homeland. I wish I could have asked him, that I had taken the time to enquire. He told Jonny and me that the only way off the streets was to be educated. So, we stole books and picked up discarded papers, and learned to read. With each new word, I discovered a thirst for knowledge. I yearned for adventure in foreign climes.

That night it all came crashing down, though. Heedless of the need to portray my toughness to the world, tears sped unerringly down my cheeks and washed away a layer of dirt.

The shout went out. "*Polícia*! Shoot out."

I can still hear the put put sounds, and smell the gun smoke which lingered momentarily in the air as bullets rained down indiscriminate of their target. In as much as if they lived on the streets, they *were* a target.

"Run," DC urged me.

"Jonny, I can't leave him."

"Go, Pedro. I will see to Jonny."

I ran; self-preservation strong. DC had taught me well, but not well enough because I paused. Hidden behind a blue Ford Galaxie, I watched DC gather Jonny to him, shielding him while a spray of bullets peppered them both. A filmy cloud of smoke filled the air. Their bodies jerked while shot after shot sprinkled down on them. I saw the blood gushing, until finally, their tortured bodies fell inert to the ground. Two lifeless figures, I didn't need to go to them to know that they were dead, but I went all the same. The need to pay my respects drove me forward, but the sight up close was far worse than it had been from my hiding place. The pale, gaunt faces, bulging fixed eyes, and the fountain of blood which flowed from the multitude of wounds haunted my dreams.

The Exiles – England

Carolina

"We can't stay here forever; surely the threat must be over now?" Her impatience showed in her finely arched brow and the tone of her voice, which he knew too well.

"*Minha querida*, I would that this is true, but while my brother is still alive we will not be able to return."

"We are not a threat anymore."

"We will always be a threat. Daniel vowed he would get word to us when we can return."

"How do you know if Daniel still lives?"

She knew better than to question Daniel's loyalty. Her husband never allowed a bad word to be said about him, but Carolina had learned to trust no one. A rush of guilt washed over her as she saw the effect these words had on her husband. A kind man, this exile was not of his making.

Carolina's body stiffened at the memory of that night buried just below the surface, pushing its way back up to the fore. Her husband's arm slipped around her shoulder. She knew deep down that he was attempting to prevent the nightmare claiming her mind again; but knowing that and stopping it were two different things.

Chapter Two

Jose

After leaving the terminal building, a wall of heat had hit me, making it hard for me to breathe, but I knew I would acclimatise in time. A driver then led us out to his waiting car; our family name had been displayed on his board to make it easier to find us. Air-conditioning blasted from his white limo giving us a welcome respite from the intensity of the heat. In the minute it had taken to walk to the car beads of sweat dripped down my face and made my shirt cling to my back. I watched with avid curiosity as we drove through the city. The noise and clamour filtered in from the streets. People talked and laughed in a way that I hadn't experienced back home.

In England, buildings were bland, brick work was red or brown, one would even see gunmetal grey in the concrete builds of the local council estates, but here a riot of colour abounded. Even on the shanty town. The poverty we glimpsed shocked me but there was also a romanticism in it which drew me. Rich smells seeped through the closed windows of the car, causing my stomach to growl as though asking for a taste.

The hotel was like a gilded prison. Everything I could ever want was here, yet what I really wanted was to go out and have a look around. I wasn't an outdoorsy kind of boy, but I'd never left England before, and Brasil seemed exotic.

"You cannot leave the hotel room, Jose. Do you understand me?" Father asked.

Did he think I was stupid? I couldn't help asking the question. "Why?"

"Why? Because it is dangerous, and you might get killed. That's why."

"Why did we come here if it's so dangerous?"

"Do you not care to see where you have come from? To learn about your heritage, the land of your forebears…"

I didn't interrupt him to point out that I could learn nothing cooped up in the hotel.

A tall man with a moustache arrived. At first I thought he was a work colleague of Father's, but as soon as he arrived, he was ushered into the living room with Father and *Mamãe*. I was given strict instructions to go to my room and not to leave.

I left. Of course, I did.

This was in the realms of an adventure, and even a boy as studious as I yearned for some kind of excitement. It would seem that eavesdropping on my parents and their guest was the height of the excitement I could expect, especially now that I was supposed to be confined to my room.

"*A twin—*" the words fragmented and I couldn't pick out the rest of what Father said.

Who is a twin? I wondered, only mildly intrigued.

"We need to find him." A few more words floated through the closed doors. I was about to walk away, as I didn't think it would be of any real interest to me, until the next words I heard halted my retreat. *"My son…"* More words were muffled; maybe Father suspected that I was listening. *"..we have to find my son's twin."*

My hand rushed to my mouth to cup the gasp which would have given me away. *I have a twin? How? Why?* A maelstrom of thoughts cascaded around in my brain. *Why would Mamãe give up her other son?*

"What can you tell me about the twin?" The unfamiliar voice could only be that of the moustachioed stranger.

"Nothing. We adopted Jose from the Dominguez Orfanato do Bebê just off the R. São Clemente when he was only a week old. We didn't see his twin after that."

Adopted? I'm adopted? My head spun. I wanted to run to the bathroom to throw up but was stayed by the stranger's next question.

"Can I ask why you only took one of the babies?"

"My wife does not have a strong constitution. Having one child to care for was all that she could cope with. So she picked Jose."

23

She picked me? She picked me, but left my twin. Do I have a brother or a sister? I wanted to scream, to burst through the doors and confront them for their duplicity and for the cruelty of leaving my sibling behind. My hands curled into fists with a longing to drive them into my father's face, to pummel him until he was bruised and bloody. A combination of fear of his imposing presence and the fact that I'm not a fighter kept me rooted to the spot.

"So, you don't know whether he was adopted?"

"No, as I said we didn't see him…"

"Yes, yes. This does make it hard. If he was adopted, he could be anywhere in the world and if he wasn't…"

Him. I have a brother. The next words the man uttered left me spinning out of control.

"If he wasn't?" Father prompted.

"He will have lived on the streets. Only the toughest and luckiest survive the streets, though. I'm sorry."

Not waiting to hear any more, I gathered up some money and stuffed it into the pocket of my jeans. I hesitated only long enough to grab the cheese and bread *Mamãe* had set aside for me. Although I wasn't hungry, my brother might be. It didn't occur to me that I

24

wouldn't find him. I had a brother, but not just a brother—the other half of me.

The realisation dawned on me like a bolt of fork lightning flashing through a stormy sky. *Mamãe had chosen wrong; she'd picked me, the sickly one, and that is why Father despises me.* Following swiftly on this thought came the most disturbing one of all. *They want to find my brother so they can swap me.* I knew *Mamãe* had not been happy for a while, but she would do what Father required of her. He would leave her with no choice. Though I knew she loved me, she would transfer that love to my twin. *Will she mourn my loss?*

My body trembled. *How will I adjust to living on the streets after having lived a life of luxury?* My brain had not computed yet that my twin could *also* have been adopted. I understood what *Mamãe* had once described as instinct. It had seemed a strange concept before, but now I understood it. That feeling which had always been with me I could now comprehend. As though I were not whole, but part of a puzzle, with a piece missing. My twin was that missing piece. *Does he feel this way, too?*

I closed the door to the hotel room using all the stealth I could muster so as not to alert my parents. *Are they my parents? Can I call them that?* Maybe if they weren't planning to replace me, I could have accepted their position as parents in my life. "Fernando and Christina." The names seemed alien, words I knew and had heard, but had never uttered. I tried them on my tongue, enunciating them with a crisp English diction before changing to a Brasilian accent. One of my hidden talents – or at least hidden from Father – was the ability to mimic people, their dialects, within minutes of hearing them speak. My ears seemed to pick up the intonation and take it in, transmitting the sounds from my ears to my mouth. I wondered what talents my brother possessed. Hopefully they would be ones that would impress Father.

I never imagined that I would have real adventures beyond the ones I devoured in books, those tales of intrepid boys who did not hesitate to throw themselves into risking life and limb.

I crept along the corridors fearful of discovery. It would be easier once I'd escaped the hotel grounds. The main foyer posed a problem. The wide open space was empty with the exception of the green liveried receptionist. The only way to get passed was if I went barefoot, as my shoes would make too much noise on the marbled floor, or if someone created a diversion.

My luck was in.

A family of five arrived with a flurry of activity. More cases than I had seen at the airport accompanied them, and their loud, brash voices echoed around the marbled space. I took the opportunity to slip unnoticed through the revolving doors while the doorman brought in the remaining bags.

Beads of sweat formed on my brow almost as soon as I stepped out from the comfort of the air-conditioned hotel and into the sweltering heat. Struggling to acclimatise my breathing brought on a coughing fit. I needed to keep moving, though. It wouldn't take long before *Mamãe* and Father – Christina and Fernando – discovered my absence. Not that they would care. It would save them the trouble of having to get rid of me. *Would they have dumped me on the streets, or would they have placed me in the care of others?*

Now that I was outside, I felt a tremor of fear. It that been one thing to charge ahead whilst leaving the hotel, but it was quite another being outside in the hustle and bustle.

Pedro

"Pedro, wake up."

I felt a sharp kick to my side and couldn't understand how Chico had got so close. On the streets we slept with one eye open, and yet, I had fallen into a deep sleep which could have resulted in me not waking up. Since losing Jonny and DC, I'd been wondering what reason I had for going on anyway. One couldn't call this living, it was existing, and what did I want to exist for?

Sometimes I saw glimpses of another life when I hung around outside the fancy tourist hotels or happened into an area where the rich frequented. There was a three-tiered system, the rich at the top followed by the working man, who was marginally better off than those of us at the bottom of the scale. They worked hard, long hours, and had a roof over their heads, but the downtrodden look they wore told me their lives were tough, too. Although, I would have sold my soul to sleep in a bed without having to keep an eye open at all times.

DC had found a vacant house, abandoned when the occupant had died and left it empty for a few weeks. Jonny, DC, and I stayed there for five days, topping and tailing in the big bed. The soft mattress was the height of luxury. DC said it was one of the things he missed most about his former life. Jonny and I knew no different than the streets. We would often go to sleep with the sound of DC's voice relaying a story of his former life, beyond our comprehension, but not our imagination.

"Pedro, I have a job for you," Chico's whiny voice intruded on my thoughts.

I pushed myself into a sitting position, rubbing the ache in my back and the filth from the streets off my shirt simultaneously. "What is it, Chico?" I gave the impression of disinterest even though I could not afford such a luxury.

"Detective Inspector Martinez said there is an American family recently arrived at The Excelsior. Stinking rich. He wants you to liberate them of as much of their valuables as you can while they are here."

"Why me, Chico? Why not you?"

"Everyone knows you are the best. He doesn't want them to know it's happening at the time. If they don't see the crime, they can't report it."

Pedro heard the jealousy infused in Chico's tone of voice. "What do you get out of it, Chico?"

"Me?"

"Yes, you, Chico. Don't play stupid. I know you'll get your share."

"Then why ask?"

"I do all the hard work and take the risk, yet you and Martinez get the best cut."

"You know the score, Pedro. You'll eat for a week."

"And if I choose not to?" I don't know what got into me, pushing like this when we both knew I would take the job or I wouldn't see the day out for refusing.

"I wouldn't if I were you. Detective Inspector Martinez says he'll arrange another drive-by shooting. We haven't had one since Jonny and DC died."

With the tell-tale stirrings of my anger rising, I wanted to rail against Martinez's authority. Wanted to kill him for the murder of my family, but I knew that no one survived on the streets without his say so. Instead I nodded, my sullen expression telling its own story.

"Pedro, you have to forget them and put their deaths behind you."

Forget them. No, I will never do that. I will make a show of putting their deaths behind me, but one day…

I nodded again. Chico was not to be trusted. He would've sold his Granny if he had one. I think he was always jealous of Jonny and me, for having DC looking out for us. No one cared enough to look out for him. Martinez used him, as he did us all, and he would slit Chico's throat without hesitation if he suspected that Chico was of no more use to him. There were two distinct types of street urchin. I fell into the former category, who believed in the code of conduct where you looked out for one another. Chico fell into the latter,

31

where nothing was sacred and if pushing the knife into our backs meant he would eat for a day, then he wouldn't hesitate.

"Alright. Out with it, Chico." The words got stuck in my throat but I forced them out. "Tell me more about that American family?"

After drawing closer to the Excelsior, I took up hiding in an alcove across the street where I wouldn't be seen. *Pivetinho* weren't noticed unless they made a nuisance of themselves. Well, maybe that wasn't strictly true.

I remembered an article in a paper which I'd rescued from a bin. "*Well done, Pedro.*" DC had been pleased and we'd taken it in turns to read the articles. It was Jonny who read how the tourists who contributed greatly to our economy didn't like to see us on the streets. Our presence made them uncomfortable. I remember thinking how great it must be in their countries if their children didn't sleep rough. "*Things will change now,*" DC had prophesied. He'd gone on to explain how they would round us all up now, and care for us in orphanages as they should. We'd protested that we didn't want to leave DC, since they wouldn't allow him into the home with us.

Things did change after that, but not in the way DC had thought they would. It was then that the police began their intermittent drive-by shootings.

I waited. Patience was something learnt on the streets; there was always a lot of sitting around. Crouched low, I hunkered down trying to ignore the smells emanating from the food vendors. My stomach craved sustenance. Pushing these thoughts aside, I concentrated on the job at hand. Distractions couldn't be afforded in this game. It was only a matter of hours later that I saw the family leave the hotel, the *mamãe* and *pai* with their three blond, tanned children wearing clothing which screamed tourists. Their clothes alone could feed me for a year. It occurred to me that I could steal one item from them and not tell Martinez. Even as the thought entered my head, it left, because I knew his spies would be keeping tabs on me.

Leaving my hiding place, I snuck into the concealing shadows. A couple excited the hotel, both well-to-do, maybe English or American, but with South American heritage written all over them. They looked around. Moments later the *policía* arrived and then disappeared into the hotel with the wildly gesticulating couple. The *policía* must use a more soothing tone with them than they do with us. Visitors had no fear of what the *policía* would do to them. Tourists had no apprehension regarding direct attacks from the *policía*. The irony was that the robberies enacted upon these favoured tourists all stemmed from the corruption within the force. Don't get me wrong, we would still have stolen from them, as it is the only way we could stave off starvation. Theft statistics would have been lower, though, as one small pick of the pocket would have fed us for a long time. What the *policía* arranged—organised crime—was an altogether different animal. It was the result of greed, not the need to feed.

I followed the family at a safe distance so I could pick my location well. It would be quiet with few people around to witness it. Not that I would get caught; Chico hadn't been exaggerating or feeding my ego when he'd said I was the best. That was the simple truth.

The Exiles – England

Leandro

The men gathered together were an unruly looking bunch.

"How is she?" A scar crisscrossed the speaker's face.

Leandro shook his head. The demons had laid claim to his wife again. Tears had coursed down her cheeks, Carolina no longer able to silence the screams which rent the air, leaving her gulping for breath as she tore clumps of her once beautiful hair out. What hair she and alopecia hadn't destroyed, now came through prematurely grey and coarse. He pictured his wife as she had once been— youthful, with a pink hue in her smooth olive cheeks. Luscious brown locks the colour of rustic wood, the smile that once illuminated her face when she saw him.

Lights dancing in eyes which had been buried under a dull, lifeless stare these past dozen years.

Nor had Leandro come away unscathed. His face was lined from worry, and his body, like hers, scarred from battle. Pleasure was something for other people, or another time.

"So, what are we going to do?"

"Can we hide out here forever? Should we not go back and expose the truth?"

"And risk our lives?"

"Is that what we're doing, living?"

A murmur of agreement spread like wildfire around the little group of men.

"We came here, exiled ourselves from our homes, and some of us our families, so that we could formulate a plan and expose the corruption in order to reclaim our former lives—what is left of them. But here we are in this cold, wet country twelve years later, and no closer. We are still only talking. I say the time for talking is over."

Leandro nodded, his comrade's sage words stirring him. He would find out what had become of his sons and his friend Daniel. Maybe then Carolina would find some joy; he just hoped it wasn't too late.

Chapter Three

Jose

The streets were dirtier than anything I had ever seen. A riot of colour was evident from the proud Brasilian flag flapping in the gentle breeze to the bright and exotic clothing worn by the women. They reminded me of the peacocks I'd seen when *Mamãe* had taken me to the zoo.

With every step I became aware of an undercurrent, a tremble of danger vibrating in the air. The screaming *put put* sound made me jump and I nearly wet myself. Realising the sounds were not that of gunshot as I'd feared, but that of a car exhaust backfiring, I laughed at myself for the foolish paths my thoughts had taken. I was being influenced by Fath…*Fernando's* doom-filled words. I could no longer trust him. His was not the truth of a father, but the lies of a man about to dispatch his adopted son to the far reaches of the earth in order to replace him with a replica. A replica who would be robust in health and who would enjoy, and excel, in the pursuits thought to make a man of boys. *Mamãe* would not be able to influence this new son. A tiny part of me hated this unknown brother set to replace me. He would make Father proud where I had failed. Yet, how could I begrudge him when he was not to blame? More than anything, I wanted to meet him.

Aimlessly I walked, caught up in my thoughts and unaware of my surroundings. My wandering had turned me around so many corners that I couldn't have found my way back to the hotel, even if I wanted to go. With this dawning awareness came fear. I had no sense of direction; back in England I was never allowed out alone. A pang of homesickness seized me while I contemplated the home I'd never see again.

I pushed on; the streets were becoming more crowded. People jostled each other, and I shied away from their contact. Perhaps it was my imagination, but the crowd seemed more menacing, less civilised. I shivered despite the blistering heat. My steps slowed as I placed one cautious foot in front of the other. There was no other choice but to go on now. The streets were twisty and winding, like a rabbit warren or something out of the Shire from *The Hobbit*. I thought of Bilbo Baggins' reluctant adventures then remembered he'd had friends with him, and a ring that made him invisible. My task didn't involve reclaiming Dwarf gold from a fire-breathing dragon, but it was equally daunting. Until this moment, I hadn't considered that my twin—should I even find him—might not be welcoming. *Hardened from street life, would he resent me for the luxurious life I had lived? Or would he teach me everything I needed to know in order for me to survive in his life?*

A commotion in front of me caused my mind's meanderings to cease. A tall, lanky boy stood before me holding a broken bottle, the edges jagged and lethally sharp.

After taking two steps back, I hit a barrier—of the human kind. Hoping to be saved, I spun around and found myself looking into a pair of glacial eyes, the lightest shade of blue–almost opaque. A vile smell emanated from the pair of boys who'd boxed me in. Both wore shorts and t-shirts, more like rags, barely held together by any material.

"Give us your money, rich boy." He waved the bottle in front of me, the sharp edges slashing the air. He hawked up and spat a huge glob of green phlegm down beside my feet.

"I– I– I have no money…" I started in English but switched to Portuguese when I saw their confusion. Looking him square in the eyes, I wasn't being brave; indeed, I feared I would shame myself with tears, or worse.

"Pedro?" The boy was looking at me, confusion written all over his face. "Where'd you get those smart threads?"

Staring back at him, my own expression was blank.

The menacing boy who'd been behind me, came around me laughing, and then patted me on the back. "Pedro, you had us fooled. Why are you slinking about in the shadows? Oh, do you have a target in sight. I heard

Chico brought you a job to do. You must have done well."

It took a few more seconds for me to comprehend. My brain was working with the slowness of a penny drop 'em machine at the fair, one coin pushed another until they all came tumbling out of the slot. *Pedro's my twin. They think I am him. Which means they know him. He is alive. Do I tell them? Or do I play along?*

"So, are you too good for us, Pedro, now you have fancy clothes?" The way his cold eyes pierced into me and his eyebrows snapped together menacingly, I knew I could not fool them. Not for long.

"I'm not Pedro."

"What games are you playing now, Pedro? Why the posh voice? We know who you are."

They took a step closer and their rancid breath washed over me. Dirt was ingrained in their pores, and as they came closer, the smell which came off their bodies made me heave. "My name is Jose," I rushed the words out to stop their progress. "Pedro, I think, is my twin brother. I was adopted. I knew nothing about him until today. I heard my adoptive parents talking. I came

41

looking for him, and until you mistook me for him, I did not even know his name."

They weighed my words up. I could see the cogs turning in their brains as they exchanged excited glances.

"You can come with us. We will take you to Pedro."

My newly acquired instinct warned me about going with them, but I couldn't see how to refuse and still walk away with my life intact. I walked along, flanked on either side by the pair who reminded me of the ugly stone grotesques used to bookmark a gate to ward off evil, and to frighten. Never had I come across anything before which scared me more than these two.

I shot surreptitious looks in their directions. The taller, gangly boy bore the signs of the pox. His skin was mottled and layers of dirt sat in and around these scars, as entrenched as the marks themselves. The other boy, with the ice cold eyes, had hair curling into the nape of his neck, thick black curls glistening like they were coated in oil.

"So, Pedro has a brother. He never told us."

"He wouldn't know. We were separated as babies. What is he like?" Curiosity made me swallow the lump of fear lodged in my throat.

The boys looked at each other and shrugged. "He's Pedro," they both answered.

I realised the stupidity of my question; I was asking two uneducated boys an educated question. My brother, too, would be without learning. How will Father deal with that? *Will Pedro be a quick learner?* Though I wondered at their age, I daren't ask. They may not know. I would estimate them to be a year or two older than me.

They led me with confidence and knowledge through the rabbit warren of interlocking alleyways. The shanty towns I had viewed from the car no longer seemed romantic. Filth and squalor were everywhere I looked. No longer seeming bright and cheerful to me, the vibrant colours were now garish and frightening. This country was so foreign to me, and I longed for the simplicity of England. Fear settled in the pit of my stomach. I didn't know where they were leading me, but the atmosphere was dense, like a thick, impenetrable fog.

Maybe they would murder me.

That they knew my brother, didn't mean they liked him.

Pedro

Only an amateur rushed a job such as this, so I took my time.

I watched.

I followed.

With three children around, I had to be more careful. Five times the chances of being caught. The children scampered ahead. It soon became clear their destination was Copacabana Beach. I had lived my whole life next to the sea, yet never had the luxury of playing in the sands or splashing in the water like I saw the rich children and tourists doing now. The truth was, I couldn't swim and I feared the large expanse of water. DC had gone there regularly to bathe, and Jonny had joined him. I always declined, saying there was little point in bathing, but I envied them and would not admit my fear. I suspected DC knew as he would nod but say nothing. DC had possessed an uncanny ability to read the truth in every situation.

The sun shimmered on the crisp blue of the sea, thousands of diamonds sparkling on the surface. A smile crept across my face at the memory of DC's story about the king of the sea, whose treasures had been plundered and for all time they now twinkled on the surface. The feel of the sand between my toes felt strange, the grainy particles clung to my feet.

The tourist children ran to the sea, squealing in delight while their parents set out towels and weighted them down.

I don't know how long I waited, but it felt like forever in the heat of the midday sun. Even under the shade of the palm tree, the sun penetrated the leaves and singed me with its temperature. There were not many people here right now. The locals would come down later, when they had finished work, and the sun was lower in the sky.

My opportunity came at last when the trusting couple wandered down to join their children in the water. Martinez wanted no trace of a crime left, so I couldn't take the wallet or even empty the contents. After glancing around to ensure I was unobserved, I made my way on silent feet to the site of my intended crime. My own resilience was praiseworthy given how the sand burnt the soles of my feet. I remained steadfast and resolute, though. The man half-turned, making me freeze. It was better to be still so that my movements weren't caught in his peripheral vision.

Jonny and I used to play the game of Statues when we were young. DC would decide on the winner. I was better than Jonny and would always be the real winner, but so as not to hurt Jonny's feelings, DC would declare him the victor half the time. Jonny was so pleased with himself at these times that I didn't correct him. DC always rewarded me with a smile of approval.

I crept forward again when the man turned back to the children. When I reached their belongings, I hunkered down and took a small wad of notes from his wallet. It might confuse him, but he wouldn't be sure if he was short, because surely a thief would have stolen everything, right? I moved away with equal care. I couldn't risk being caught now. This family would be rich pickings, and Martinez would reward me well.

Chico met me the moment I left the beach, no doubt the weasel-faced toad had followed me.

"What took you so long, Pedro? Are you losing your touch?"

"Chico, a crime which is no crime takes precision, and for that, you need patience. If Martinez had thought you capable, he would have asked you."

His mouth opened, flapping like a fish stranded on the shore. "He doesn't risk his best men," he shot back.

I snorted, derision bringing this idiot back to Earth with my words. "You, Chico, are expendable. We all are. He doesn't warn you about the shootings because he doesn't care if you are killed," I snapped out, pleased that I had wounded Martinez's pet, but also aware that he would exact revenge when I least expected it.

Chico had no moral code.

In exchange for the notes, Chico handed me fifty *cruzeiros* and a note instructing the market seller with whom he traded to provide me with a steaming bowl of *Moqueca* every day this week. I headed back home with a full belly and a coin, albeit a fairly worthless one, in my pocket. I also had my instructions to repeat the exercise tomorrow for the same reward.

Pietro and Luiz stood in my doorway. It appeared as though they were waiting for me. Their faces lit up when I approached, the gaps between their rotten teeth showing as they tried smiling on for size.

I nodded at them. My mouth was dry and the muscles in my body tightened. My hands, behind my back, balled into fists.

"Pedro, we have a surprise for you." Luiz's pale eyes bored into me.

"You can keep it, boys. I have no need of surprises."

"A nice surprise, Pedro," Pietro asserted, his smile making me feel like I might be sick.

"Really, guys, that is very kind, but I have no desire for surprises."

"No desire for surprises," Luiz mimicked, causing Pietro to cackle. "That education has made you a bit uppity. You'll like this one. Come on out, Jose."

Taking up a fighting stance, I tensed for an attack. Flight would be useless; they would have covered my escape routes. *I would fight despite being outnumbered. Even if I hurt one of*— I gasped. Before me stood an exact replica of me. Something stabbed into my chest but it wasn't a weapon. "Doppelgänger," I choked out, careful not to make eye contact. It surprised me when I heard him laugh.

"No, Pedro, not a doppelgänger. I'm your twin."

I started to deny the existence of a twin, but stopped. A feeling, not quite a memory, but something I couldn't explain, triggered an acceptance of his words.

The Exiles – England

Leandro

It was decided that one of them would go back and scout. They couldn't all go back blindly, they needed to know what danger they were facing.

"Your brother has never met me. I have a new name, new identity, false papers. No one would ever trace me."

"We all have new identity and false papers," Leandro argued.

"My face won't be recognised," Stefano asserted.

A vote was cast, to which everyone except Leandro agreed.

"You would throw yourself under a sword to achieve nothing, man! Stefano is the right man for the job. Or would you take all the glory for it?" Leandro knew Teo used these words to stay him. No one, with the exception of Daniel, knew him better.

"Leandro, it is a fact-finding mission. I will go in and uncover the information we need, and then feed it back to our group. It will be my honour to serve," Stefano said with an air of pride.

The men spent the next hour debating how Stefano should do this, and what information was required.

"Please, if you can find out—discreetly, of course—about Daniel?" His tone was pleading.

They all shifted uncomfortably in their chairs, being of the same opinion as Carolina, but no one said anything.

Chapter Four

Jose

The boys, whose names I discovered to be Pietro and Luiz, led me to a slum. Flea-ridden bundles of rags spread into the corner of an archway in an alleyway. Small, perfectly round holes potted the building in a random design.

"He'll be back soon. This is his home."

I looked around and tried to keep the disdain from crossing my features but knew more discerning characters would have spotted it with ease.

"He'll get such a surprise." Never had such innocuous words been imbued with such threat. My lips wobbled while I valiantly fought the appearance of tears.

"Why don't you take a seat?" Pietro indicated something I assumed to be Pedro's bed.

"No, it's okay. I don't want to invade his space, not without his permission."

"You're his brother, he won't mind." When I didn't move, Pietro added, "I'm telling you that you can."

That wasn't an argument in favour, as I didn't believe anyone should enter his home, such as it was, without Pedro's permission. The menacing look Luiz gave made me shrink back into the shadows, grateful to be out of the sun. Hunger rumbled in my stomach making me think about the food I'd put into my rucksack. There was no way I could eat in front of these boys, who doubtless won't have eaten in—I couldn't quantify how long they would had gone without. I almost offered it to them but knew there'd be nothing left for Pedro.

It would have been better if I had gathered a few more things together before fleeing. Maybe I could have taken some more money, too, although the thought of stealing from my par—well, from 'them,' was untenable. Maybe it wouldn't have been so much as stealing, though, as taking enough to eat, only taking what they would have been paying for my food.

I didn't have too long to wait, although it felt like a lifetime. Thoughts cascaded through my head like the little ball spinning around a roulette wheel, bouncing in and out of the slots.

"Stay back, Jose. Pedro is here. Let's surprise him."

It was the most surreal moment of my life so far to see my mirror image staring back at me. His clothes were ragged and he wore a layer of grime like the others, but in all other ways I could have been staring at my own reflection. Pietro and Luiz's reaction to me should've warned me, but somehow I was not prepared.

This day, which had started with me as an only child staying in a luxurious hotel room, had led me to the slums where I discovered my twin brother with the knowledge that I was adopted. For the first time, I realised I knew nothing about my real parents. *Had they given Pedro and me up, or had they died?*

Stepping forward, I watched first the shock, and then the disbelief chase across his face. He looked as though he suspected some kind of trickery.

"Doppelgänger." The last word I expected him to say.

"No, Pedro, not doppelgänger. I'm your twin."

My brother wasn't uneducated. I could hear it in his enunciation, and doppelgänger was not a usual run-of-the-mill kind of word. It was one that I'd just learnt myself.

The flicker of something flashed in his eyes, and I asked, "Do… do you remember something?"

His brown eyes, almond-shaped and almost identical to mine, looked back at me with an expression that I couldn't fathom. "No, I don't remember anything."

I knew he was lying.

"Okay, boys, you can do one."

"Don't we get a reward? A finder's fee?"

"How about I don't slit your miserable throats while you sleep?" Pedro moved menacingly towards them, and they scarpered.

Standing stock still, I was undecided whether to follow them. For a fee, they would take me back to the hotel. Now I had met my brother, I wasn't sure who I should be more scared of. I noticed his bare feet and cringed knowing the roads I had traversed to get here had been hard going, cobbled with loose stone chippings and a layer of rubbish, and I was wearing shoes.

"Have you lost your tongue? I asked what your name is."

Stammering out an apology I then told him my name. *Can he read my thoughts?* Twins were renowned for being able to know the thoughts of the other, but did that just apply if you grew up together? With more bravery than I knew I possessed, I asked him why he had lied to me.

He took a step closer. "Why do you say I lie?"

Backing away, I said, "You said you remembered nothing, but I think you do."

A thoughtful expression crossed his face and I realised he was sizing me up, and deciding whether to give an honest answer or to lie again.

"I didn't lie. I don't remember anything, but I did get a feeling. Maybe a familiarity?"

I nodded. "Can I ask you a question?"

"No one's stopping you."

"How long have you lived on the streets? You are clearly educated."

"Straight in at the serious questions, then. No small talk." He hesitated and I guessed he needed a chance to gather his thoughts. "Come, join me in my humble abode."

Sitting down, I tried not to show my hesitation to rest amongst the filth. I pictured Father's face and then, without faltering, made myself as comfortable as the setting allowed.

"I wasn't adopted by a family…" He went on to tell me about being looked after by a man called DC, and his adoptive brother Jonny.

I didn't know what to say. My sheltered life had not prepared me to deal with the appropriate response.

"So, now you tell me? What of our parents? What are they like? Why didn't they want me?" A break in his voice betrayed his emotions.

He had so many questions that needed answering but I didn't possess the answers. "Pedro, I can't tell you anything about them. I was adopted."

"Did your adoptive parents not tell you anything about them?"

I paused. How much could I confide in him about what I had heard? It was too soon to share my fears. I didn't want him to know that they'd chosen the wrong one, what a disappointment I was. "They didn't tell me anything. They don't even know that I know. I overheard a conversation today. They said I was adopted and that I had a twin. They were talking to someone else and explained that *Mamãe* couldn't have coped with two babies, which was why they only took one."

His jawline clenched while he digested this news. "Why you?"

Shaking my head I admitted that I didn't know, had no more answers.

"Are you hungry?" I asked, remembering the food in my bag. I fished it out and handed it to Pedro.

Pedro took it from me, then broke it in two and handed me half. This little gesture told me a lot about the manner of person my brother was. Despite being in this slum, I felt happier than I ever had before. I had a brother. I was no longer an only child.

Pedro

After the initial shock of finding out about my brother, I experienced a range of emotions. DC and Jonny had been the only family I'd known, and yet, here before me was a blood brother *and* the possibility of finding out who I was, where I'd come from, and why I had ended up here.

I dispatched Pietro and Luiz with threats of violence. Maybe it wasn't the wisest thing. On the streets you had to be tough, but you also didn't invite enemies. Friends helped, while enemies created issues later on down the line. You never knew when you would need someone.

I felt numb. I had thought after losing DC and Jonny that there was no room in my world for sentiment. Caring for people only got you hurt. This identical copy of me standing opposite me was my flesh, though. We had shared so much, growing together in our *mamãe's* womb, and then what? His adoptive parents had kept him, and thrown me away as though I were rubbish? He intrigued me while making me hate him all at once. My head hurt. Life on the streets was black and white, so I didn't understand these thoughts. Maybe he would have his use, though.

It surprised me when he challenged me with the accusation of lying. There was more to him than a boy who tried not to show the tremble in his body, but his wide eyes gave away all his secrets. Although we exchanged stories, I was no nearer to knowing where we'd come from.

I envied him the privileged life he'd lived. However, there was something sad about him which seemed to go deep. Jose hadn't confided in me. I'm not sure why I thought he should. We might have the bond of blood, but we knew next to nothing about each other at this point.

"So, do Fernando and Christina know you are here?" His head lowered into his shoulders, and he shrank away, giving me the answer. "Won't they be worried?" Thinking of the couple with the *polícia* at the hotel, I pressed, "Where are you staying?"

"The Excelsior."

"I saw a man and a woman there earlier, with the *polícia*. They looked really worried. I can take you back there now, if you want?"

"No. I came to find you. Can I stay for a while?"

His answer reinforced my earlier thought that he was holding back. He would tell me when he was ready.

"It isn't an adventure on the streets, Jose. It's real. I can try to protect you, but I can only do so much." My heart twisted at the thought of harm befalling him. Was it possible to care so soon after meeting a person, or was this the result of our blood bond?

He nodded. "Will Jonny and DC come here, or do they sleep elsewhere?"

I had left that part of the story out, not wanting to share something so personal with a stranger. There was something endearing about my brother, childlike and innocent, and I decided to trust him with my innermost pain.

"Jose, when I say the streets aren't safe, it's not just the other *pivethino* you have to worry about. Starvation is a factor, too, but there is also the *polícia*…" I hesitated when I saw the look on his face.

"The police are there to help you, Pedro. Father always tells *Mamãe* and me that if we are ever in trouble, we must trust the police to help and protect us."

I snorted; his ignorance was not his fault. "Maybe in England or for respectable families."

"DC read from the papers once that tourists couldn't bear to see children living on the streets. They criticised the Brasilian authorities for allowing it… for not stopping it. So the *polícia* did something. Or at least they went some way to reduce the homelessness on the streets. The *polícia* organise all the local petty crime. They pay us to commit the crimes. It's enough to feed us, sometimes, but not to get us out of poverty or off the streets. They tell us who they want targeted. That is why I saw Fernando and Christina at the hotel. I was given my orders to steal from an American family—"

"Were there five of them?" he interrupted me.

"Yes, that's them. Do you know them?"

He shook his head.

"The *policía* control everything. They take money from the tourists but they don't get their hands dirty. We do. If we don't, we starve—but the tourists aren't happy seeing us. Local businessmen, they don't like us either. They think we should all be annihilated. So, the drive by shootings started."

His eyes dilated wider than I'd ever seen on a person, and I wondered whether they would pop out.

"I was resting one night with Jonny. We used to sleep on the main strip in one of the shop fronts. Jonny wasn't well. Despite my efforts to get us food, it was getting harder. When I did, he was too ill to eat more than a mouthful. He had no strength. One of the lads ran past shouting that the shootings were happening. I tried to help Jonny. I really did. DC told me to run. He said he would help Jonny get away. I didn't get very far before hiding behind a car. It was a blue Ford Galaxie. I'll never forget it. DC had stooped down and was picking up Jonny's skeletal frame when I heard the squeal of brakes, the popping sound of the guns. Then I saw the bullets spraying them. They stood no chance." I sobbed, allowing myself the luxury that I hadn't before.

His arms enveloped me. I held myself stiffly for about thirty seconds, and then succumbed to his wordless support. Any doubts that Jose was my twin were swept aside in that moment when our souls connected. I knew I had felt this before. Somewhere in the recesses of my brain was a memory which wouldn't form, of a time before that we had comforted each other—either in the womb, or when we'd been ejected into the cruel world that had separated us. It must have been the latter, as I was sure our trials had only begun when we entered the world.

We sat huddled together in silence. I felt no shame in my emotions, no need to pretend feelings or to put on an act. My twin knew who I was just as I knew him. It was the minutiae of our lives we needed to fill each other in on.

"Let's get some sleep," I whispered and then realised that Jose was already snoring. I eased him down so that he was lying, and then covered him with the scant rags of my possession. I didn't have silk sheets or wool blankets, but I would share what I had with him. I was no longer alone.

The Exiles - England

Leandro

The bullet ripped through his chest a split second after he watched, powerless, as Carolina's body contorted and fell forward before she hit the deck.

Leandro woke up dripping in sweat. Even after twelve years, the memory was vivid. Thinking about it had triggered the dream. He looked across the empty space of bed and remembered he had signed Carolina into the psychiatric wing of the hospital. When she had her episodes, there was no way that he could care for her. He had tried in the beginning, but she was sneaky; the disorder of the brain made her so. She'd waited until he slept and then began her patterns of self-destruction. They were criss-crossed over her once unblemished skin. Knives and scissors were locked away. Leandro went to the barbers to have a shave as the razor was too dangerous if she got hold of it. It was surprising to learn how many everyday objects could be used to mutilate the body when the desire was strong enough.

The scars ran across Carolina's body like the intricate map of the London Underground, and like the trains, her scars went deep down, too. The bullet had not only almost taken her life, it had left a visible mar on her olive skin and a large indelible mark on her brain. It had also taken away her chance to have any more children, and as such, she hungered for the two they already had, desperate to hold them again.

Leandro shook his head once more and wiped away the solitary tear gathered in the corner of his eye. It was time he got up and ready for work. He would make his daily visit to Carolina when he had finished.

Chapter Five

Jose

When Pedro told me about DC taking him and Jonny under his wing and looking after them, I thought I had heard the worst there was to tell. To me, this was way more horrendous than my own world being turned upside down. How could I tell him of my own trivial worries?

Hey, Pedro, I may not get to live in the lap of luxury anymore. It may be your turn.

Through his eyes, I experienced the streets. His warning that it wasn't the adventure of boyish imaginations was loud and clear. The hard floor pressed through my clothing. *How can he sleep here?*

He offered to take me back to the hotel, but despite the warnings and the discomfort, I knew there was nowhere else I belonged. Oh, don't get me wrong. If I could take Pedro back to the hotel with me, without the threat of our separation, I would. I didn't have an idealised vision of the streets anymore, certainly not since meeting Pietro and Luiz.

What he told me next, I didn't want to believe. In that moment, my whole childhood was stripped from me. What I viewed to be good or bad became jaded. In my innocence, I'd believed everything that had been told to me. There was no time to dwell on my own inadequacies as Pedro told me about the brutal murder of his street family. If DC hadn't sent Pedro away, he, too, would have been killed.

A cold shiver swept through me. I didn't want to pay credence to his words. Even though I didn't want to, I had no choice. The evidence was in the rumble of emotion, the quiver of his words and the tears running down his face tracing a path through the grime. His shoulders shook, his thin body wracked with grief. I held him as *Mamãe* once held me when I was upset. The embrace we shared triggered a whisper from the past, a past I knew nothing about.

I awoke covered in rags and disorientated until memory flooded my consciousness. A coughing fit followed, leaving me weak. My back hurt from the hard floor but then I heard the other half of me, and it all faded.

"Are you okay, Jose?"

I smiled, followed by another coughing fit.

"Are you ill?"

"A weak chest." I tried to smile again even though my chest was tight.

"What aren't you telling me, Jose? Do you not trust me enough to share with me?"

"I don't know what you mean?"

"There is something you're keeping back from me. I can hear it in your voice, in the words that you're not saying. What haven't you told me? Are you ill? Is that why you're here?"

I realised having a twin was going to mean I wouldn't be able to keep my innermost thoughts hidden. Now there was someone who was tapped into me.

"My fath– Fernando has never been proud of me like a father should. I am not sporty, or strong. I am bookish, a nerd they say in England. I always thought I took after *Mamãe*. She used to say I had her constitution, but I can't have, can I? Because I was adopted. *Mamãe*… Christina and I have always been close. We're both sensitive. I've always disappointed Fernando; he never admitted it, but I could see it in the pinched lips and hard stares he gave me. I heard him say once that Christina had made the wrong choice. I never understood what he'd meant by that until yesterday, when I overheard snippets of his conversation. I heard them say I had a twin and that they needed to find him."

Pedro stayed quiet, his brows inverted. "Why are they interested in finding me now?"

"Because they made the wrong choice, and I have been a disappointment. So they are going to swap us."

Pedro gasped. "That is cruel. I should not be surprised, but somehow I expected that your adopted

70

parents must've loved you lots to have taken you from the beginning. How could they not continue to love you?'

"*Mamãe* loves me. She is so proud of me. We love to spend time together. We play, we laugh, and we talk. I share all my confidences with her. Or I did. She shares things with me, too; things she knows Father wouldn't approve of. She calls them our delicious secrets."

"Won't she stop him, then?"

"Nothing and no one can stop Father once he has made his mind up. *Mamãe* says he is like a tank rolling over everything in its path."

"Tell me more, Jose? Paint me a picture of your life."

We talked for hours as I told him about the details of my life. The things I liked, the people I'd met and what I enjoyed.

"One day *Mamãe* took me to this really expensive hotel for afternoon tea."

Pedro's eyebrows drew together as confusion crept into his expression.

"It is like a tradition in England. You go and have delicate sandwiches where the crust is cut off. The bread is soft and white, almost spongy in texture. They are cut into little triangles, very delicate for the rich folk. Then there are the array of cakes, and scones with sultanas, which you have with clotted cream and jam. There is so much that you feel sick afterwards. The adults have champagne but they give me orange juice. When no one was looking *Mamãe* held the champagne glass to my lips and let me have a sip. It was all bubbly and tickled my nose."

It occurred to me that this was maybe not the best story to tell a boy who had never had enough to eat, but he seemed entranced. Every now and then he interrupted to ask me about something he didn't understand. Pedro had the same thirst for knowledge as me.

"Fernando and Christina are rich, Pedro, but you must understand there are levels of rich. There are people whose prosperity goes beyond any comprehension. When we go out, we 'people watch.' We try to imagine who they are and what they do, and what kind of life they live. If we can hear them talking, I mimic them. As soon as I hear the nuances in a voice or an accent, I can recreate it."

"Show me?" Pedro's eagerness was childlike; he seemed younger than our years. It saddened me because I knew he had not had much fun in life.

"I will, Pedro, I'm just getting there." I laughed. "So, this couple came in. She was wearing a fur coat. *Mamãe* said it was mink, and that even with the good money that Father brought back, it would cost a week's wage. When the woman allowed the waiter to take it, an evening dress that skimmed her body was revealed, and *Mamãe* said that to fit so well it was couture—especially made for her. Diamonds the size of ten pence pieces sat in her ears and on her fingers, too." When I demonstrated the size, his eyes widened as I'd known they would. "The one on her neck was twice the size. When she spoke to her husband, she said, '*My dear, it is quite beyond the pale that you have brought me slumming it here.*'" I mimicked her voice, and Pedro's high pitched tinkle of a laugh made me chuckle—I'd expected it to be more... more manly.

"That's not all, though. Her husband replied, '*My dear, you cannot call the Ritz a slum, and you know very well that Mother favours it, so please don't say that to her. She does still hold the purse strings to our inheritance.*" This time I imitated the man's plummy voice.

"What did she say?" Pedro had tears streaming down his face while he leant forward cupping his face, entranced.

The honest answer was I couldn't remember any more of the conversation, but I didn't want to disappoint him. So, I weaved a story of them being tied to his mother until, on her deathbed, he would inherit.

Pedro lay back contented, hands behind his head, and I followed suit taking up the same position. Together, we laid there in silence, not feeling the need to break it.

Not until Pedro heard a sound that is, and told me to hide under the bundle in the back of the recess.

Pedro

For the first time since losing Jonny and DC, I woke up with a sense of purpose. I knew I wouldn't be able to keep him in my life forever, nor did I want to. I didn't want my brother to experience the brutality of the streets, to learn the lessons in life I had. I wanted to preserve as much of his innocence as possible, for as long as I could. I regretted the harsh lesson life had taught him last night, when I'd told him about DC and Jonny. I should have fabricated some tale of a tragic accident.

We spent the morning talking. He told me stories of life in England, a life I couldn't imagine, of people who wore rocks on their ears which could feed every orphan in Brasil for life. I loved the way he spun his stories. How, for a while, I could have been right there with him as he allowed me a glimpse of another world seen through his eyes.

When he mimicked the rich couple, I laughed out loud, while in my head, I, too, tried the sounds out. I didn't dare try them out loud in case he mocked me. I didn't know which of us had been born first, but it felt as though I were the elder. Maybe that was because of my experiences.

We lay back in companionable silence. Closing my eyes let me imagine us both somewhere else. Somewhere beautiful, where we could just be two brothers playing, getting into mischief, and fighting as brothers will, but going home with our clothes scuffed and dusty to be scolded, fed, and bathed by loving parents.

The light slap of bare feet against the cobbled stones alerted me.

"Hide, Jose," I urged. Until I knew who it was, I didn't want to expose him to any danger.

He had just burrowed under the pile of blankets and clothes when Chico's weasely face showed up in my doorway. It was good I had made Jose hide. I knew I couldn't keep the existence of my twin a secret for long, since Pietro and Luiz knew of him, but maybe I could work out a plan to get him back to his cocooned world.

"Pedro."

"Chico, what can I do for you? Two days in a row. Are you here on Martinez's bidding?"

"Detective Inspector Martinez said you did well yesterday, but the American family have so much more to give."

"Okay, Chico. I'll go soon."

"I'll go with you."

"No need. I don't need an escort. I have some other business to take care of. No point in delaying you. Important person like you must have lots to do."

The burro burro didn't recognise my sarcasm. Eager as Chico was to be thought of as someone important, he was happy to lap up the praise. I waited until he was gone before instructing Jose to stay where he was until I got back.

"Are you stealing from that family?" The muffled words came from beneath the layers of cloth. I heard disapproval, and for the first time I felt shame for what I was about to do.

"It is the only way we will eat, Jose. I don't have rich parents who give me everything on a plate," I snapped then stalked away, angry.

While walking through the streets, I realised that my anger wasn't aimed at Jose, it was at myself. I longed to have this job over and done with so I could apologise. Hopefully, he wouldn't do anything stupid in the meantime.

The streets were alive with the buzz of people; locals and tourists merging together. The smell of burritos floated sweetly on the warm air. My mouth watered imagining how it would taste, it had been a long time since I'd had one. The street vendor kept a watchful eye out for the likes of my kind—ragamuffins intent on stealing his food. Maybe I'd ask Martinez for burritos oozing with refried beans, cheese, and meat as my payment. The thought made me smile.

I was in luck and didn't have to wait long for the family to leave the hotel. They seemed to be creatures of habit; but then, most people were. Again the children walked in front of their parents, who kept a watchful eye on their young.

The sound of Jose's disapproving voice echoed around my head. For the first time I saw this family as actual people, instead of being impersonal targets. Viewed through Jose's eyes, they were victims of a crime I was intent on perpetrating. I'd never personalised a target before or thought of their feelings, but now it unsettled me. Shaking my head, anger dripped from me like rain from a sodden umbrella. I didn't have the luxury of conscience. If I didn't steal, I didn't eat, and neither would Jose now. Thinking about the threat of another purge of 'street scum,' as Martinez liked to call us, made me shudder. I had to do this job then get Jose back to safety. Switching all thoughts off, once more I became the consummate professional.

Today the family were browsing the shops, and I would have to be extra careful. I did a mental risk assessment of the situation. While this would be an ideal pick-pocket scenario, Martinez wanted no contact. The shopkeepers, who saw me as a threat to their potential sales, would be a hazard. Plenty of shoppers, both locals and tourists, would also be prospective witnesses. It wouldn't be too hard for me, though; I relished the challenge.

What will happen to Jose if I get caught?

I pushed this thought aside and sidled up to the family, walking close enough behind so that I could hear their conversation, but not close enough to be suspect. Yet again I thanked DC, as though I were thanking God, for having taught me English. In fact, DC had been the only God I could believe in. It had started out as a game. DC had said by the time I was his age, I would be proficient not only in Portuguese, but also in English, Spanish, French, and Italian. I think educating Jonny and me helped him preserve a little bit of his old life.

"Bring me back some dinheiro and a new word in any language. The first word you remember and can repeat will be the first language you learn." DC had laughed so much that tears had coursed down his cheeks when I'd handed him a wad of notes and repeated, *"Money."* At first, I'd struggled to get my mouth around the harsh foreign sounds, but I'd waited, bemused, until his mirth subsided. He'd then explained to me the meaning of the word, dinheiro.

I smiled at the memory.

"Pamela, the clasp on my watch is loose. Let me know if you see a watch repair shop."

I almost laughed out loud. If there was a heaven then DC would be looking down on this, and his sides would be hurting from laughing. This was too easy. My heart rate increased until the pounding against my chest and the blood pumping in my ears sounded a deafening cacophony.

He didn't even notice me walk up to him, shadowing closely.

Funny to think someone wouldn't feel something as substantial as a watch slide from their wrist. But he didn't. I timed it to perfection, disappearing into a side alley seconds after palming it. Increasing my pace now, I was eager to be away. The cold metal in my hand was heavy. I knew from experience this meant that it was worth something. Maybe Jose and I could eat like kings for weeks on this. Martinez owed me.

I slowed down to a casual pace after turning into the winding, interlocking *aléias*, which were an ideal place to relieve a lost tourist of their belongings while they floundered around like a fish on the end of a fisherman's hook. Some gave chase, but my speed, agility, and knowledge of these lanes gave me the upper hand when that happened. I'd never been caught, although I had come close once. Jonny had saved me by biting the man who imprisoned me with strong arms, and then we'd both scarpered. I had no doubt that Martinez would *not* protect me, should I be caught.

Shivering, I thought again of an ex-convict's words, stories of a prison life which made life on the streets sound like the equivalent of the hotel Jose had described.

The Exiles - England

Cafe owner

Cigarette smoke wreathed its way above the heads of the cafe patrons. The cafe owner walked through the haze he'd grown accustomed to after twenty years of business. A non-smoker, he had long since adapted to the smell permeating his establishment, including the living quarters upstairs. His wife grouched continually that it wasn't good for the children. But then, his wife grouched about everything. Her current complaint was about living above a greasy cafe. She didn't complain about the cafe when she spent her generous allowance, or the little stipend on top of that which he allowed her for personal women's luxuries. When she claimed she needed such things to help her stay beautiful, he'd bite back the retort that she had never had beauty to start with. He wouldn't have been lying.

No, he didn't concern himself with the cigarette smoke.

In the last ten years or so, this had been a regular haunt for the group of ex-pat Brasilians whose patronage had stopped him from going bankrupt. The half dozen men came in daily, drinking thick, black coffees. It was rare that they ate, but their presence attracted others. No one frequents an empty food establishment. People think if no one is inside, it means there's a problem. So, slowly, his trade had built around this little group until he had an enviable list of regulars.

He often wondered what these men discussed, as their intense conversations were all spoken in Portuguese. He kept promising himself that he would learn to speak the language, but another year had gone by, and he still hadn't.

Today, the men stopped talking when he deposited their coffees in front of them. That wasn't normal. He wished again that he had learnt, because he was sure that what he would hear would be a tasty morsel of gossip. He wondered whether they were dissidents plotting anarchy, attempting to overthrow the government. As a boy, his imagination had been sparked by stories of 'The Gunpowder Plot' and Guy Fawkes.

Another regular came up to the counter ordering half a dozen take-away bacon sarnies, some with egg, some with sausage, but all with brown or red sauce. With some reluctance, he drew his attention from the group to take the order.

Leandro

"Any word from Stefano?" Leandro asked as soon as they had all sat down at the table.

"Leandro, he has only left today on a plane. You know how long the flight from England to Brasil is."

Leandro's mind wandered back to the long flight he had taken with Carolina. Both barely recovered from surgery, the flight could have caused a relapse. By the time they had landed on English shores, their skins were as pale, if not paler than, the natives.

"Leandro. Leandro?"

"Hmm, what?"

"Are you okay, my friend?" Teo asked.

"Yes, yes. Just miles away."

Chapter Six

Jose

As soon as the words were out I realised they'd sounded like a reprimand. I knew what Pedro did for a living, and while I couldn't say I approved of theft for theft's sake, I understood he had no choice. My concern was for his safety, and if I were honest, I feared for my own as well.

Beneath the pile of rags I lay still, like a child playing musical statues—a game I'd won time and again as I wasn't, by nature, a restless person. Soon I began to notice a rancid smell emanating from the bundle. The way the scent filled my nostrils made it difficult to breathe, so I pushed a tiny gap into the material, which cleared my nose, and breathed in the… I hesitated to call it clean air. Another smell floated on the wind. The appetising aroma of food drew a loud growl from my stomach. I prayed no one was walking past at that moment, for they would've surely heard the noise which, to me, sounded as though a canon had been fired.

The passage of time was excruciating. I had no concept of how long I was alone, but it felt as though days had gone by. Being in the dark the whole time only reinforced the feeling as dread filled my empty stomach. *What will happen to Pedro if he's caught? Surely they don't hang criminals here, do they?* Certainly not children. However, tenacious doubts crawled into my head while Pedro's recollection of the shootings that had taken his friends' lives haunted me.

Every sound I heard filled me with foreboding. The slap of feet against the paving divided my thoughts. *Is it Pedro? Am I about to be murdered as I lay here defenceless?* I pictured the tears *Mamãe* would cry, and then thought about how it would serve Father right, for wanting to trade me in.

"Jose, are you there? It's me, Pedro." His gentle voice and the delicious aroma of food assaulted my overwrought senses all at once.

"Pedro, you're safe. I'm sorry." I burst from the pile of rags.

"Why are you sorry? What did you do?" His voice had a wary edge.

"I made you angry."

"No, Jose, you didn't. I understand how you feel. It is not a profession I want to be proud of, but I have no other options open to me."

"I know. I didn't mean to sound disapproving. I was scared for you…"

He threw himself down beside me and handed me a burrito which smelled, and tasted, more delicious than anything I'd ever tasted before.

"Tell me about it?" I asked whilst munching on a mouthful of food.

"Do you really want to hear?"

"I will have to learn sometime if I am to live on the streets."

So, Pedro told me how he had stolen from the American family for a second time. How he had crept up behind them waiting for a clue, some piece of information which would help him. It had seemed as though chance or destiny had placed the watch in his lap. Maybe God was on his side after all; maybe He had guided Pedro's hand.

I thought of the fabled Robin Hood who stole from the rich and gave to the poor. It was a tale I loved, a part of English folklore and its heritage, passed down through the generations to be told and retold. I recounted the story for Pedro.

"No one ever cheered the Sheriff of Nottingham. Robin was the hero with his band of brigands."

"He sounds like Detective Inspector Martinez," Pedro said with his mouth full.

"That would make you Robin," I replied, feeling a fierce pride in my sibling.

"Jose, you can't live this life. You have to go back to your family."

We'd just found each other and he was rejecting me already. When I saw the worried look in his eyes, the way his brows drew together and the little lines that crossed his forehead, I understood it was out of concern for me.

"Pedro, you *are* my family. I do want to go back, but not if it means without you. Maybe they will take us both in, if I explain that I found you?" Even as I uttered the words, I knew the falsehood in them. I was torn. While I didn't want to live out in the streets, it was unbearable to think that, after finding Pedro, I could lose him again.

"Jose, we both know that won't happen. They did not want me then, they won't want me now."

"They don't want me, Pedro. Remember they came here to swap us."

"What if…" Pedro stopped. "Wait, let me think… what if we change places? I become Jose and you Pedro. As they plan on swapping us, it won't be for too long. Then, when they do the swap, you will be back with them and I will stay here."

Pedro's idea to change places was genius, or it would have been, if we could find a way for us to stay together, and yet, deep down, I knew he was right. I needed to go back.

I knew Pedro didn't think it could happen, but I told him I'd get work as soon as I could, and then I'd fund him to come to England to live. I would start with my pocket money; no longer would I fritter it away on trivialities, books, and comics. There was the local library for books, and why did I need comic book heroes when I had a real, live, flesh and blood one in the form of my brother?

Hours passed while we talked. I told Pedro everything about my life I could think of. At least, anything that would apply to him while he was pretending to be me. It occurred to me that once we swapped, I would not know how to be with *Mamãe,* because surely I could no longer have the same bond, the same relationship.

The meticulous attention to detail Pedro showed in the plans he made and the questions he asked gave me a glimpse of what he must be like when he was out stealing. When I asked him whether he would teach me how to steal, I was relieved when he said no. He would let his friend Carlos in on our secret, and enlist his help to look after me.

Did he think me a child to need babysitting? This thought was followed straight on with relief as I contemplated how alone and vulnerable I would be without Pedro's protection. This reinforced my resolve to ensure I would work hard to get him off the streets.

When it came time to exchange clothes, it was a big moment, much more than the mere swapping of cloth. It was significant as I took on the mantle of a boy living on the streets and he assumed my life of privilege. I taught Pedro how to talk like me; he had a natural ability for mimicry, too. Perhaps it was in our genes. A tear welled in the corner of my eye; we should have had a lifetime together but we'd been separated, and now would be again.

We played a game to help him take more in. I pretended to be someone—the couple from the Ritz, Fernando and Christina—and he copied me. We laughed so much that it hurt, but still we continued.

Pedro

When I'd returned with the steaming burritos and saw the blankets quivering I knew Jose was scared. It made me realise how much I needed to protect my brother. Jose was not cut out for street life. He would be caught the first time he tried to steal, if his conscience even allowed him to try in the first place. My brain whirred trying to make a plan, but all I could come up with was that he had to return to Fernando and Christina. Nausea swept through me at the thought of losing him so soon after he had found me, but better that than watching him go in the way Jonny and DC had. I shivered. His innocent belief that he could persuade them to take me on sparked an idea of how I could help him.

I outlined my idea of me going back to the hotel as him while Jose stayed on the streets as me, then when

Fernando and Christina swapped us, we would be back in our natural homes. I was rather pleased with my brainwave.

Though Jose wanted to argue with me, he acknowledged the truth, which was that he wasn't cut out for street life. "I will get a job as soon as I am old enough and I will send for you."

I smiled, pleased with the sentiment, but knew that would be many years away and I might not survive so long on the streets. Each day was borrowed time here. I didn't tell Jose that, though. We made plans, talking long and hard. I allowed him to develop the fantasy.

After a while I moved onto practicalities. He had to tell me everything about his life I needed to know in order for me to pull off the pretence.

"What is your favourite food?"

"Burgers."

"What don't you like?"

"Sprouts… *ew*, yuck."

We talked through the afternoon, and into the night, until the early hours of the morning.

"So, will you teach me how to pick pockets so I can eat while you're away?"

"No, Jose. It isn't something I just tell you how to do. I'm going to leave you under the wings of a friend of mine. He is one of the few people who I can really trust on the streets. Martinez owes me a weeks' worth of food. I'll let it be known that I'm laying low as I am unwell, and will send Carlos to pick up the food. He'll take a small cut of it, but he can be trusted. By then I will ensure your parents have found you, and will swap us back."

Even as I said the words I feared for him, but couldn't see another way.

"Tomorrow morning I'll find my way back to the hotel. I will say I was lost. In fact, I will bring Carlos. I can say he guided me back for a fee. Carlos can keep half, and we will have the rest."

"We'll need to swap clothes. You will also need to practice my accent. Let's change clothes now so that you can get into character."

I had never worn anything that had felt so luxurious, the quality of the clothes could be felt as they brushed my skin. In the moment I first slid them on, I felt as if I could be anyone, do or achieve anything. We discovered that I, too, had a natural flair for mimicry, or at least I did once I'd got past my shyness and no longer feared seeming stupid in front of Jose. We rolled around on the floor, laughing while we imitated people he knew or had met until my belly ached. I found it easy once I allowed the nuances to sink in.

"Here's one I heard on TV—"

"Whoa, there," I interrupted. "What is TV?"

"Oh, yes. I didn't think about that. Oh, how can I describe TV to you?" He scratched his head, a look of pure puzzlement creasing his forehead. If it were that hard for him, how would it be for me?

"Okay… no… what can I say?"

"Maybe a literal description to start?"

"Okay, if you can imagine a box…" He showed me the dimensions with his hands. "It runs off electricity. You know electricity, yes?"

I nodded. "What does it run?"

"Okay, do you have playhouses here? Or theatres where people act out a story?"

"Yes. I haven't been to one, but DC told me about it. Maybe it is a bit like carnival, no?"

"Loosely. Well, the TV has actors in it playing parts—telling stories."

"They are in the box?" Incredulous, I showed Jose the dimensions that he'd first demonstrated. "How can that be?"

He laughed. "They, the people, are not inside the box. It is filmed and transmitted through cables to the TV." Jose pointed at the cables running across the city overhead.

"You're having me on? Come on, Jose, you must think me stupid."

He shook his head and tears were rolling down his face.

My brows furrowed together. "I think… I might… there is a shop, on the far side of town which I don't go to often, and they have… that's it, that's what the TV is." I beamed realising that I had seen them just not known what they were.

Jose fell backwards clutching his sides. He tried to talk but the words wouldn't form as he was so weak from laughing, but then he started coughing. The coughs seemed to wrack his whole body as he brought up green phlegm.

"Are you alright, Jose? Do you need a doctor?"

I was relieved when he shook his head as I had no means with which to secure the services of a doctor.

Laying there that night, fear trickled into my brain like veins threading their intricate way through a body. At first, I'd imagined the idea of the swap to be an adventure, but the more Jose told me, the more my fears increased. How could a boy from the streets, who knew nothing about living in a real home, pretend otherwise? *What is the worst that can happen if they discover me? I have no choice if I want to protect Jose from the harsh realities of my world.*

When Carlos arrived the next day, I could see from the surprised look on his face that word hadn't travelled about me having a twin. He looked from Jose, to me, and back again.

"Pedro?" he asked and looked at Jose.

The exchange of clothing had worked.

"Carlos."

I could almost believe Jose was me when he switched to the sounds of a Rio de Janeiro *pivetinho*. Roaring out loud, tears formed in the corner of my eyes. I hadn't laughed or cried so much in my life, as I had in the last few days.

"I am Jose Sanchez. I am Engleesh."

"No, you are English, not Engleesh," Jose corrected, and Carlos looked so startled I feared he was on the verge of running away.

"Don't worry, Carlos, you're not going crazy. I am Pedro, and this is my brother, my twin, Jose. Jose was adopted and only just discovered he had a twin. He came to find me." I stopped to allow Carlos—who despite being kindly, was not the sharpest tool in the box—the chance to digest it. I filled him in with a basic outline, and then told him of our plan.

"So, you want me to say I saw you on the street, lost and scared. You asked me to take you back to The Excelsior, which I promised to do for a small fee, *não?*"

Jose and I exchanged looks; we'd explained it three times already.

"Yes, Carlos. Perfect. You must also let it be known on the streets that I'm not well so that you can get the food from Martinez."

He hesitated. "What should I say is wrong with you?"

"Anything. Vomiting or—"

Jose interrupted, "No, it can't be that or you wouldn't want to eat. What about measles or something? No one will want to come near for fear of catching it."

Carlos and I chorused a horrified, "*Não!*"

"The fear of something like that spreading through the streets is enough for someone to drive a knife in you while you sleep," I went on to explain.

Jose blanched, losing all semblance of colour.

"Maybe a chest infection, *sim*? You already have a bad cough."

"*Sim*, Pedro, you had a bad chest yourself last year, remember?" Carlos added, triggering the memories of DC's tender care of me during that time.

The Exiles–Brasil *Twelve years earlier*

Leandro

Leandro and Carolina left the hospital with tears in their eyes from having to leave behind the most precious things in their lives, two beautiful, baby boys. Leandro's arm curled around his wife's shoulders, supporting her. She shouldn't have been out and about so soon after giving birth to the babies, but he knew that was not the reason she needed his assistance to keep her walking forward. His heart was heavy, leaving the twins was the hardest thing he'd ever had to do, but he knew for Carolina it was worse, having carried and nurtured them during the nine months of her pregnancy. Above the noisy beating of his heart, Leandro heard the clicking noise and spun around, Carolina following suit. They both caught sight of the gunman who'd planned to shoot them in the back, but the bullet was already whistling through the air and had slammed into Carolina before they could react.

Leandro whispered Paolo's name, but the shot with his name on it was already whinging its way toward him. His arm sagged as Carolina's weight dropped. When the bullet connected and threw him backward, the pain was unlike anything he had ever experienced. The second the cartridge impacted with his chest, his brother had turned and fled through the warren of *favelas* which connected Rio, not even staying to watch him fall. Leandro's body hit the cold, hard ground, jerking as it made contact. He was vaguely aware of being beside Carolina but couldn't move to check whether she was alive or not. Leandro had no concept of time and it only seemed like a second before he felt strong arms curve under his back and his knees. Through hazy eyes, he saw Daniel as he was lifted up.

"Carolina," Leandro gasped, expelling a painful breath with the words.

"Teo is with her, my friend. We'll get you both to a doctor, to Sebastião."

Leandro meandered in and out of consciousness only just aware of the car journey. Every bump in the road caused an inordinate amount of pain which jerked him awake again. The further out of the city they got, the worse the state of the roads were, and the pain became excruciating. He tried to speak but his mouth was dry and his throat felt as though there were sharp blades slicing him.

"Hush, my friend, save your strength." Daniel's voice trembled.

"My boys," he whispered. "Twins…" No more words formed as wave upon wave of pain shook his frame.

Leandro became aware of Carolina's pallid face although his vision was blurred, and he feared the worst. Her utter stillness and silence didn't bode well, either.

"Is she?" He gasped, his throat gurgling from the effort.

"No, she still lives," Teo answered.

They arrived at the surgeon's house. Sebastião, who was a personal friend of Leandro's, opened the door to them. However, even he hesitated for a fraction of a second when Daniel and Teo stood on his threshold with the bloodied mess of the couple he and his wife had entertained only the week before. Leandro was barely conscious in Daniel's arms. He would have slipped under had Daniel not kept talking to him, insistent that Leandro attend his words. The last thing Leandro remembered was being carried into the house and taken to one of the bedrooms where Daniel placed him on the bed.

Sebastião

Sebastião viewed his best friend Leandro, and his wife, with horror. The thought crossed his mind that his family's lives were at risk if he helped them. This was replaced straight away by shame, of course he would help them. He owed Leandro a blood debt, plus a lifetime's friendship alone guaranteed that he would not turn his back on him. The surgery wasn't easy, both patients had lost a lot of blood and moving them, although Daniel and Teo had no choice, had been risky. Carolina was also weak too from childbirth. The complications were many and he had minimal equipment at home. He couldn't even dispatch anyone to get him additional supplies. The risks were too great. However, he was a renowned surgeon, one of the best in the whole of Brasil, so they had a fighting chance.

It was many hours later that he finished operating, instructing Teo and Daniel to help stem the blood flow, and to sponge down the feverish bodies of his patients. Exhaustion was something he was used to in his profession, but the stakes were higher here.

"The next forty-eight hours will be crucial. We have done all we can do now. Their lives are now in the hands of Deus. We can only pray for them now. And hope they have a strong will to live," Sebastião told Daniel and Teo before also telling them they should take it in turns to watch over Leandro and Carolina for he needed to sleep now.

Leandro and Carolina stayed in Sebastião's home for a mere two weeks, but that was enough to make him jump at every sound. Sebastião was fearful the authorities would hear of the assistance he had given the fugitives and that his family would be threatened—or worse. He didn't fear for his own life, but his wife and four daughters were his world. Even so, he protested when the false identities arrived and Teo and Daniel insisted the flight, which had been booked for England, had to be caught.

"They're not up to travelling, they need to be stronger."

"It's not safe for them to stay any longer. You have done well, but their lives are in our hands now."

"Wait. Ten minutes please." When Sebastião came back, he bore an envelope in his hands with a note, which he handed to Teo. "Look after this for Leandro."

"What is it?"

"It's a letter for a solicitor who holds the wherewithal to access a bank account. There's ten thousand pounds in it, left to me by a distant relative. I am deeding all of it to Leandro and Carolina. They must have the accompanying note to claim it." He watched them leave with fear in his heart but a sense of relief.

It took many months before he stopped looking over his shoulder or dreading a knock at the door.

Chapter Seven

Jose

I lay still the whole of the night, unable to sleep while the silent but relentless *tick-tock* of time marched toward daylight. The nearer it came, the more intense the dread, fingers clenched around my heart and squeezed. I could feel the tightening in my chest.

"Carlos will be here soon," Pedro said when the first rays of sunlight spread into the darkest reaches of the archway. "We will see if he can tell the difference. Although he isn't very bright."

It wasn't long afterward that a small, wiry boy, who looked about fifteen, arrived. He had the beginnings of a growth of stubble. He looked from Pedro to me, and back again, eyes dilating. There was something innocent in his face despite his obvious years living on the streets.

We filled Carlos in, bringing him in on our plan and making him an accomplice in our duplicity. We exchanged a conspiratorial smile when Carlos finally understood what it was we wanted.

With each passing minute came the growing foreboding. I had been left alone here once before for a few hours. I had no idea how long this would last, but knew it would be longer, significantly longer, with no way to mark time other than the dawn of day and darkness of night.

My terror was emphasised as we planned what illness Pedro would have to keep him away from the *polícia*. My thoughts returned to Pietro and Luiz, who'd put the fear of God into me during my first encounter with the streets of Rio. Thoughts of being stabbed in my sleep ran through my head like a record player stuck in a groove on a LP.

"I should go now." Pedro looked at me, and I knew he was thinking the same thing as me. "I will get you to England, Pedro, I promise. I will send for you."

"I know," he said the words, but I wasn't convinced he believed them.

I will show him. Even as I thought it, I knew it would be years, not weeks or months.

I stood before Pedro and opened my arms, pulling him to me for a hug. With false cheer we engaged in hearty back thumping. Pedro pulled back first and then turned, walking away without a backward glance. I wanted to call out to him, to beg him to stay, but I stayed silent. As I watched him go, it felt like I were being rent in two. A solitary tear made its way down my cheek.

My throat tickled, and again I was attacked by an uncomfortable coughing fit. I had underplayed my illness to Pedro, but this had been with me for the last six months and it didn't seem to want to shift. *Mamãe* had taken me to the doctor, who had then sent me for all sorts of tests and lots of blood samples. At the end of it, *Mamãe* had told me everything was fine but that I must take things easy.

It had been about that time *Mamãe* and Father started whispering. When I walked into the room conversations stopped. A week or so later they told me we were going for a holiday to Brasil. It must have been then that they decided to get rid of me. *Mamãe* was clearly saddened, as she kept hugging me.

I longed for a hug from her now.

A rustling noise disturbed my thoughts. I sat rigid, images of knives and guns in the hands of both street orphans and police cascading through my head. I closed my eyes. Whatever was about to happen, it would be better if I didn't see it. I could still hear the scrabbling sound, and it was coming closer. I peeked out of one eye, unable to contain my natural curiosity. The other eye popped open when I came face-to-face with a rat who was better fed than the humans around here. I tried to shoo him away, but he sat on his haunches and looked at me. *These things have no fear.* After what seemed like minutes, whereby the rat won the game of staring me out, it scarpered as another sound approached.

I lay down. If I was going to pretend that I was ill, then I should look as though I were resting.

"Pedro."

My heart made the noise of a dozen horses thundering toward the finish line. I was certain that my heart beat was audible, and that the ground on which the weasel-faced boy stood, trembled.

For a nanosecond I ran through the descriptions Pedro had given me of the people I might encounter. I started to cough. At first it was deliberate, but then it triggered the dry cough which was never far from the surface. This gave me a few more moments to open up the filing cabinets in my brain containing the stored information.

"Chico…" I gasped, partly due to the coughing but also with relief that I'd opened up the right memory drawer. "Not well," I croaked.

Chico stepped back, fear in his eyes. "What's wrong with you?"

"Oh, just a cough, but it has left me weak. I must rest."

"Detective Inspector Martinez wants you to do another job. The Americans again."

I started to cough again, fearful I might be forced to do this job. "I can't stop the cough. There is no way I would not attract attention. Det–Martinez wants there to be no trace, *sim*?" At the last second I remembered Pedro always referred to him by Martinez, and hoped I had done right.

"Okay." Chico looked uncomfortable.

Coughing again, triggering the attack on purpose, this time, caused Chico to take a step backward, obviously fearful of catching my bug. His bulging eyes seemed incongruous on his gaunt face.

"Can you pass him the message that I'm ill. I will do it if he insists, but I don't want to risk getting caught. He was clear on that." I prayed the gamble would work. *Holy Mary, Mother of God, please help me in my hour of need.* The words had never been so important as they were in this moment.

Chico nodded and hurried away, the rise and fall of his gait more pronounced than it needed to be. It reminded me of the tough boys at school, how they postured and walked as though one leg were shorter than the other. To pass the time, I decided that praying wasn't such a bad idea. I recited the Hail Mary, The Lord's Prayer, and every other prayer I had ever learned. It had a calming effect on my jangled nerves. After a while exhaustion overtook me, and I fell into a deep slumber.

The waft of food beneath my nostrils woke me. I started upon realising I wasn't alone. Carlos handed me a burrito without a word—same meal two days in a row, but I wouldn't complain—and with evident relish, tucked into his own. Pedro was right; I would never survive the streets alone. He slept with one eye open, in such a light slumber that the merest whisper of the wind or a leaf blowing down the street alerted him. Yet I'd slept like the dead, and hadn't even been disturbed by the presence of someone else. The fact that it was a friend and not foe didn't matter in this case.

After we both finished eating, I turned to him eager for information. "Did you see my parents? Did Pedro get there okay?"

Carlos chewed his last mouthful with vigour and nodded his head. He handed me some coins and showed me the same in his hand.

"Did you see my parents?"

"Yes."

Talking to Carlos was hard work. I was going to have to extract every tiny detail from him.

"How did they react to seeing me... him?" I corrected, not wanting to confuse Carlos.

"The lady, she cried and pulled him in for a hug, and the man, he held him close, too."

I felt the first stirrings of envy. I couldn't remember Father hugging me before. *What if Pedro liked it with them so much that he didn't want to swap back?* I mean if they liked him, and changed their minds. This thought, which had not occurred to me before, was now all I could think of.

Pedro

Before I left, I picked up the little parcel wrapped in brown paper and tied with string which DC had left behind. It was all I had left of him, and I treasured the contents despite never having been brave enough to open it. I allowed Carlos to guide me. While we walked along the streets, I walked a step behind. It was important that I took on the guise now, so that I would be well-versed in playing Jose. From this moment Pedro ceased to exist, or at least he did until my task was completed. I looked afresh at the exterior of The Excelsior. It wasn't the rich pickings of my life of crime. Now, it would be my temporary home, my haven.

I wondered what I should do when I went in. *Do I walk up to the front desk?* Would I have the confidence needed to ask for the Sanchez family? Would the boy clearly uncomfortable in these surroundings give away the truth?

I reached for the door and was barred by the doorman, who I had not considered.

"Go away, vermin," he addressed Carlos and me.

Help came from an unexpected quarter.

"I have brought the lost Engleesh boy Jose Sanchez home. He promised me a reward." Carlos stuck his hand out for his reward and I almost laughed.

The doorman looked at Carlos and then his eyes flickered over me. His scrutiny made me uncomfortable. My urge was to run.

"Please take me to *Mamãe* and Father." My voice, small at first, gathered strength and momentum. "They will not care to be kept waiting."

"Yes, Master Sanchez." He guided me into a glass triangle.

I'm trapped, he knows it's a lie. My chest tightened as I viewed my prison, but then it started to rotate. I took a step forward, and one more, and another until I had reached the deep red carpet on the other side. I was now inside the hallowed grounds of the hotel whose clientele I stalked to relieve them of their belongings. I longed to take the shoes from my feet as I was sure the plush carpet would be soft. The shoes I wore pinched my feet, mine were a bit bigger than Jose's.

The doorman followed me through into the next little cubicle, but had stopped Carlos from following.

"I promised him a reward, so he must come, too."

"Your parents will arrange for him to be rewarded if they wish it, but we cannot allow his type into the hotel."

You let me in and I look every bit as disreputable, albeit I'm in good clothes.

I saw the American family heading toward me. My first instinct was pure terror, thinking they had recognised me and would have me arrested. They took little notice of me; although one of the boys, a little older than me I guessed, flicked me with a contemptuous glare. I watched as one by one they entered the glass cubicle and then exited the hotel. Bang on schedule. Had I been Pedro, I would have been waiting outside for them.

At that moment I heard a high-pitched, female scream.

"Jose, *meu bebê*."

I was swept into strong yet delicate arms and held tight. The sweet smell of roses wafted up to my nostrils as I stood there stiffly crushed in her embrace. Unsure how to respond at first, because I had never had this before, I soon relaxed and wished I could stay in her arms forever. I had never known a mother, had never felt a woman hugging me. I thought of some of the other boys my age who slept with disease ridden whores, who, in return for their services, found them paying customers. Tourists who did not want the direct approach of a street woman. You could spot them easily, from the furtive way they looked around. Their wives and children thought they were on business. It surprised me, as high class whores could be attained without the filth of the streets, and they were allowed to rent rooms by the hour in the lower class hotels. No one allowed these women to cross their thresholds. Prostitute and punter could be seen pressed together in the alleyways followed by animal grunts. Some of these men paid for the services of the street boys. It was a profitable business but not one I had ever considered. Not even when knives ripped my stomach with hunger. DC had instilled in Jonny and me that death was preferable in these circumstances.

Christina finally pulled back. Hers was an ethereal beauty, a dainty face set against a luxurious length of jet black hair.

"Let me look at you, *bebê*."

I felt the presence of a dark, brooding man beside me and as I raised my eyes, my sight travelled across a broad expanse of chest, upwards to the chiselled features of Fernando.

"Father."

His hand snaked out, and I flinched from the certain blow. Seconds later, I was crushed to his chest as he, too, held me in a tight embrace. It only lasted a moment before he pulled me back and scrutinised me. I felt sure he must know I was not his *filho*.

"Don't ever do that again, *Filho*. Your *mamãe* and I have been so worried. Let's get you up to the room to bathe."

I hesitated.

"What is it, Jose?"

I pointed at Carlos through the glass. "I promised him a reward if he brought me back."

The look Fernando gave Carlos was filled with disdain, showing me a glimpse of the man Jose had described. Jose had been wrong to think Fernando did not love him, though. *So why would they want to exchange him?*

Fernando, with a flick of his hand, summoned a member of staff who sported a burgundy uniform the same colour as the carpet. Reaching into his pocket, he pulled out a handful of coins and handed them to him, with instructions to give it to the boy outside.

"He looks like he could do with some food, Fernando."

"He can buy it with the money I have given him."

"Actually, Jose, you look terribly thin. You look like you haven't eaten in months. How is your cough?"

"We can talk to him later, Christina. Enough of conducting our business in public."

I threw a last look over my shoulder at Carlos who held his hands out for the money and smiled when it dropped into his palms. An imperceptible nod passed between us.

We started to walk, moving from the deep red carpet to the shiny marble floors. I tried not to gasp at the scale of luxury. I looked down so that the widening of my eyes would not give away how in awe I was. Especially since Christina had not taken her eyes off me. She held my hand.

"I have missed you, *querida*."

I felt grateful for this contact, for the squeeze she gave my hand. It was with trepidation I stepped into the lift Jose had described. I was fearful of this moving cage. My stomach dropped down to my bowels when I felt the lurch as it began to creak and groan, moving upwards.

The Exiles - England

Leandro

"I've had word from Stefano," Teo told Leandro as they waited for their friends to join them.

"And?" Leandro expelled his breath once Teo confirmed that his brother was still alive and thriving. "Daniel?"

"No word. We know he went underground. Stefano went to see Sebastião to let him know you are still alive, and to thank him for saving your life."

Leandro digested this information. "I don't suppose…" He couldn't bring himself to finish the question.

"No word of your boys, Leandro… well, except that they're not with your brother," he spat the word out as though he'd found himself in an *Alice in Wonderland* world and had inadvertently drank from a bottle marked 'poison.'

The others arrived, and words floated in the air around him like little insubstantial bubbles. Leandro didn't hear them while he digested the information. *Does that mean my boys are safe?* A sob broke free as he contemplated the alternative.

"Leandro?" Teo looked at him with eyes full of concern.

"I'm alright, my friend."

The tears squatting in the corner of Leandro's eyes belied the falsehood in his words, but Teo said nothing. "If you want to talk—"

Leandro broke his friend's words by lifting his hand, there was nothing which hadn't already been said.

"So, now what do we do?" One of the men voiced Leandro's own question.

Chapter Eight

Jose

Carlos was not a riveting companion; he did not help the hours, or even the minutes, pass. I did feel a modicum of security in his company, though. His quiet presence was soothing, and I wondered whether his silence was due to the solitude of his existence.

"How long have you known Pedro?" *I'll engage him in conversation if it's the last thing I do.* At first he didn't say anything, and I thought maybe he hadn't heard. My mouth formed the words again, but fell silent as he answered.

"As long as I have been on the streets."

It was a start.

"How long is that?" I sensed the tension and when I looked at him, his eyes had darkened. "I'm sorry. I should mind my own business."

He nodded but said nothing, laying back.

After a while, the rhythmic rise and fall of his chest and his slow heavy breathing made me think, *He's asleep*.

"It isn't easy to calculate time on the streets, but it has been about five years."

His words shocked me, not only because I'd assumed him to be asleep, but because I'd also thought he'd lived his whole life here, as Pedro had. I didn't dare ask anything else; it was obvious that I had poked my finger into a wound which had not scabbed over.

Quiet descended on us again. Later, the buzz as the streets came to life alerted me to the coming of dawn. The wind whipped up dust swirling in the air before it settled upon us, causing me to start coughing again.

Carlos leapt to my side with a rushed, "You okay?"

I hadn't realised he could move so fast.

"Let's go and find you some water to drink."

As I followed him the coughing subsided, until only the occasional one tickled my throat. Waves of nausea washed over me, leaving me feeling weak, while I stayed close to Carlos. The nausea may have been caused by the fear weaving my stomach into knots.

We were laying and looking up at the stars, back in the relative safety of our alleyway, when Carlos broke the silence.

"My parents were imprisoned for clashing with the *policía* over human rights. They fought for the rights of orphans. They wanted orphanages to take in the street children and to put a stop to the corruption of the ones which sell babies for a sizeable profit. They were arrested while protesting. They believed that my uncle would take me into his home until their release. Two things happened, though: they were not released, and after six month's imprisonment, they both died. The official story was that they contracted a disease, but the truth is, they were beaten to death by the prison guards. My uncle decided that caring for his nephew in the short term was one thing, but taking me on for good when his sister died, was another. He already had a wife and two children to feed. I was another mouth, and all my parent's worldly goods had been seized by the state. You see the irony in the story, don't you?"

"I'm sorry, Carlos."

"S'okay. Everyone has endured hardships here, so my story is no worse than anyone else's. I have never shared it before. Actually, no one has ever asked. Nice but simple Carlos, what story has he got to tell?"

I felt uncomfortable about the truth of these words. "I'm glad you told me."

He nodded, and we lapsed into silence. In my head, I'd already decided that somehow I needed to make enough money to rescue him, too. How I would achieve this, I didn't know, but I had to do it.

We were woken the next morning by the reappearance of Chico.

"What are you doing here, Carlos?"

I could see his mistrust in the look he gave us. This wasn't the norm, so it was suspicious to him.

"Carlos came to see me and was concerned by my chest infection. He stayed to see if I needed anything. We talked into the night." The way he raised his eyebrows made me realise that Pedro wouldn't have given him a reason. "Not that it's any of your business," I added, trying to introduce a hard edge to my voice.

Chico's sharp features relaxed so I must have been convincing. My heart pounded at twice its normal rate, and I was sure he must hear it, too.

"Detective Inspector Martinez wanted me to check on you."

"Tell him I'm still weak." It wasn't a lie; my words were breathy and my head felt light. I supposed it to be an adrenaline rush. As if on cue, the coughing started again and racked my frame, leaving me weaker still.

"I'll tell him."

There was nothing as convincing as the truth.

"You had better not be here too often, Carlos," I said while watching Chico slink away.

"I promised Pedro I would look out for you."

"I know, but it is stirring up suspicion."

"I can visit you?"

"I'd like that."

Despite the bravery of my words, I was struck by the overwhelming sense of loneliness and apprehension which loomed. The day ahead stretched long before me. I couldn't venture out when I'd said I was too ill to work for Martinez. Besides, I would get lost in the maze of alleyways. Given I was playing the part of Pedro, I couldn't ask for directions. Never again would I complain of boredom when I got home.

The sound of a scuffle drew my attention. Poking my head up from where I lay, I saw two men fighting. Having never witnessed violence of any kind before, a frisson of fear raced through me. This wasn't something one saw in a leafy London suburb. The only exposure I'd had to this kind of behaviour was through American cops-and-robber type programmes, and none of those seemed real.

The taller, heavier man landed a right hook to the small, wiry man's face. With a sickening thud, his nose split open and blood gushed out. It poured down his face, splattering his clothing and hands. With a roar he attempted to land a punch in return, but the big man parried it with ease and a lightness of foot which belied his size. His maniacal laugh filled the air.

"Stay away from my wife," the smaller man yelled as though he had the upper hand, as though he had laid a blow which had put the fear of God into the perpetrator.

The giant laughed. "Your wife is a *prostituta*. She opens her legs for any man who pays her."

Rage bellowed out of the smaller man in a deafening roar. A flash of steel and the giant went down. The pavement reverberated as he hit the deck with a resounding thud. Blood spurted outward. Vomit welled up in my throat and I swallowed, trying to push it down. It occurred to me then what I'd just witnessed. I shrank back down into the bundle of clothing.

As though sensing my presence, the man turned and looked in my direction.

I closed my eyes. *Please don't see me.* Abrupt panic manifested in my trousers as I wet myself. After what seemed like an age, I opened my eyes. The only evidence the fight had taken place was the corpse lying in the street, with a bloodied knife sticking out of his gut.

Pedro

When the lift stopped, I thought we'd reached our room. Imagine my surprise when I discovered we had the whole upper floor. Looking down at my dirt encrusted body brought shame at having traipsed it through the pristine whiteness. I almost apologised for the mess that I was leaving, but stopped myself in time. *I must remember not to say rash things. Responses only for the time being.* It would be so easy to give myself away.

"Jose, go and run a bath," Fernando ordered

"Run a bath?" I repeated trying to remember what Jose had told me about the bath. I knew what bathing was, of course, but how was I supposed to run one? Standing still must have given every appearance of my being stupid.

"Oh, bless you, *meu bebê,* you look exhausted. *Mamãe* will run it for you. Actually, it might be good to shower first, to wipe all the worst of the dirt and grime away before your bath."

She led me though to a room which I recognised from the description of what Jose had called the bathroom. The room was so white, so startling, that it almost hurt my eyes. I jumped when the rushing sound of water cascading down started behind me. *Has it started to rain inside?* I didn't move, being unsure what to do next.

"Go on, Jose." She pushed me, with the lightest touch, toward a glass container which seemed to be the source of the water flow. Steam was building up. "Okay, you don't want your *mamãe* to see you naked. I'll pop outside while you undress. I'll come back in while you are in the shower. Oh, *meu bebê* is growing up fast."

I almost laughed at her assumption. It had never occurred to me to worry about being seen without clothes.

"Leave the clothes on a pile on the floor so I can throw them all out," she called through the closed door. I almost cried out in objection, but stopped myself in time. These clothes, to me, were worth money, but to them, they were dirty, and would be thrown out as such. I hunted

around for somewhere to hide DC's package. Christina couldn't find it, or worse still, throw it out with the pile of clothing.

My fear of water had to be conquered right now, so I stepped under the stream of warm water with caution. It wasn't as though it were the sea, which, to me, was a huge untamed beast. The prickling jets pelted my skin and made me flinch back out of the spray. With trepidation, I forced myself under again. It wasn't so bad the second time. Allowing the water to wash over my hair, I watched the clear water turn black on contact with my skin before it sped to the floor to be sucked down the drain. After a while, Christina re-entered the room. I could make out her faint form as she bent over the bath. More running water sounded from her direction.

"Don't forget to use soap, Jose, and scrub behind your ears."

Soap? I looked around, and after finding the only thing other than me in the cubicle, I picked up the item that must be soap. It was like a slippery fish in my hands and popped out, dropping to the ground.

After picking it up and clamping it with the other hand to stop it jumping again, I wiped it experimentally over my skin, turning it black. When I ran it under the jets of water, the dirt melted off as though it had never been there. I discovered pleasure in the scrubbing of my skin, remembering to wash behind my ears as instructed; I even cleaned inside them.

After a while I noticed dials on the wall and fiddled with them out of idle curiosity. The water turned ice cold, causing me to scream. I heard the sound of Christina's laughter which was like music to my ears. After twisting the dial again the water stopped.

The door opened a tiny bit and a hand came through.

"Don't worry, I'm not looking. Here's a towel to wrap you in, Jose. You don't need to dry off if you're getting into the bath. I have put some bubbles in. I know how much you like them." She left.

At the click of the bathroom door, I wrapped the fluffy softness around me and headed to the bath. I looked at it with suspicion. This was a bit more like the sea—well, a much smaller version. Reaching my hand in I touched the bottom. It came up to the middle of my arm, and I thought, *I'm sure no one has ever drowned in water that shallow.* Climbing into the shiny bath I was grateful not to be filthy dirty now, as I would have stained it for sure. Sinking beneath the warm water, I came up spluttering with a mouthful of bubbles, causing me to cough.

The door burst open and Christina almost ran in. "Jose, are you okay?"

"Yes, *Mamãe.* I'm fine." Lines creased her forehead, and a look I couldn't fathom darkened her eyes. My hasty reassurance seemed to work, though.

She left me alone again, this time to my thoughts. Something wasn't right. I didn't know her yet but no one reacted like that to a cough—*did they?* Jose had a persistent cough which he had dismissed as nothing. Something didn't add up, and I was sure gonna find out what it was.

"*I've laid some clean clothes out for you on the bed,*" Christina called out as I emerged from the bathroom wrapped in a new, fluffy white towel.

The magic word rang in my ears, and memories of a bed from a few years ago drew a smile from me.

"Then come on out for food."

Food. How am I ever going to be able to give this up?

Opening the door with trepidation, I almost closed it again, sure that something so big, so rich, could not be for me alone. The clean clothes spread out on the bed made me hesitate, though.

Shaking fingers picked up first the shorts, then the t-shirt, both a dark shade of blue. Holding the clothes to my cheeks, I delighted in the feel and the clean smell. They weren't brand new, they belonged to Jose, but I had never worn anything like them. Laid out also were pants, socks, and shoes. I hated the thought of putting the shoes on knowing they would pinch my feet, and restrict my freedom.

Unable to resist, I threw myself onto the bed, rolling about with abandon. I stopped at the sound of a creak in the wooden frame. *Have I broken it?* It looked sturdy enough, but I didn't want to take any chances. My desire for food was strong, but my curiosity was stronger while I pulled open doors and drawers which reminded me of the story of Aladdin's cave that DC had told Jonny and me. Instead of gold and jewels, there were rows and

136

stacks of clothes. *Surely they can't all belong to Jose?* Next to the bed I discovered a drawer full of books. I ran my fingers over the thick, hard spines in awe before placing DC's package at the bottom, under the books.

When my stomach made noises which couldn't be ignored any longer, I went out and found Fernando and Christina sitting at a huge, dark wood table with throne-like chairs.

"Come on then, Jose. We have been waiting for you. We are starving."

You have no idea.

The table groaned under the weight of the food and I nearly asked who was joining us but held my tongue. All would be revealed without me asking stupid questions. Fernando put his hands together and closed his eyes. Christina followed, so I figured I had better do so, too. I kept half an eye on the proceedings, though; on the streets you always kept one eye open.

"Lord, bless the food that we are about to receive. We thank you for your bounty…" a slight pause and then he added, "We also thank you for the safe return of our beloved son. Amen."

"Amen," Christina chorused, and after an expectant pause I grasped that I, too, was expected to close off the prayer.

"Amen." Praying was not something we bothered with on the streets. If there was a god, he would have no more interest in us than the rest of society.

"Tuck in," Fernando ordered.

The array of foods and the sheer quantity astounded me. Unsure, I watched them, allowed them to take the lead so I could see what to do with the implements in front of me.

"The manager has sent us up an assortment of foods. They thought you may not want to eat in the restaurant as usual today."

Eat in a restaurant. I quailed at the thought. *I'll face that tomorrow.*

Placing a selection of foods on my plate, unsure what most of it was, I hoped I hadn't picked anything that Jose didn't like.

"You are being more adventurous with your choices today, Jose," Fernando commented with what sounded like approval.

I found myself preening under it while thinking of poor Jose, who could not please this man. "I am very hungry tonight, Father. I think I would even eat sprouts," I joked, earning a laugh from both my parents.

When did I start to think of them as my parents? I'm just getting into the role of Jose. The way I sought to please Fernando made a lie of this. I felt the echo of my deceit.

When we finished, it didn't look as though the food had been touched so I asked what would happen to the leftovers.

"It will be thrown out," Fernando answered.

"Could…" I hesitated, but built the courage up from the warmth of his previous approval. "Could we take it to the street children?"

It was then I saw the disappointed look Jose knew well.

"We can't go out to the streets, Jose. Your little adventure on the streets is over. You will not go back there again. I forbid it!" His voice had risen to a level below a shout.

"Maybe one of the hotel staff would take it to them?" I persisted, angry now myself.

Mamãe looked at me and then gave me a slight shake of the head. She was warning me. In that moment I knew he was the reason I hadn't been adopted, the reason I had grown up on the streets.

"We gave that boy who brought you back money. It does you credit that you wish to reward him well, but it ends there, Jose. We will hear no more of this."

If I'd been Jose, I might have recognised the warming signs—the tone of his voice, his heightened colour, the stiff jut of his chin. I did see them, but I was not Jose, and my fear of this man was not as severe as the pain of starvation I'd lived through.

"Father, there are children the same age, younger even than me, who are starving. Their bones are visible, their faces gaunt, their eyes sunken into their sockets like a skeleton. They beg and steal for scraps of food or scavenge what they can from bins. This would please God, as he would see you are doing his work." I tried a change of tact.

"The Lord will provide for them if he wishes them to prosper. If, as you say, they scavenge from bins, then this will find its way to them anyway."

The dismissive tone made me want to scream at him, to shout, to stamp my feet and threaten him, but I had to remember the part I played. I rose from the table, the chair scraping the tiled floor.

"Where do you think you are going?"

"I am tired. I'm going to my room."

"Sit down," he thundered. "You have not asked for permission to leave the table. Such insolence. You have been too soft." The last he addressed to Christina.

A sob escaped Christina's lips, a sound which tore at something deep within me.

I sat down, lowering my eyes with the pretence of obedience, but I did not want him to see my blazing anger, the rebellion. For Christina, for Jose, I would say nothing. However, I developed a strong dislike for Fernando in that moment.

The Exiles–England

Carolina

"Leandro, how much longer do I have to stay here?"

"Until you are better, my darling."

Carolina nodded, hurt haunting her eyes. "Any news? Did Stefano get home?" Leandro hesitated, she saw it. "Tell me, Leandro. The lack of information hurts more than knowing ever can."

"I don't know anything… much. Paolo is still alive, but he doesn't have our boys with him."

She blanched at the name of her husband's brother. Her eyes showed the pain, but soon clouded as she had learned to hide so much from her husband. "And Daniel?" she asked, an afterthought. It was proof that she was thinking straight.

He shook his head.

They lapsed into a silence that wasn't the comfortable state of a couple married for so many years. It was the silence of lies and half-truths a couple who love each other use to protect the other, but it cannot sit easily despite the good intention.

Half an hour later they both breathed a sigh of relief when Leandro stood up to leave. He bent down and planted a tender kiss on his wife's forehead, and squeezed her arm in a show of support.

"We'll have you better and out of here soon," he whispered.

Carolina stood up on legs shaking like a new-born colt and wobbled to the door. A white-coated man approached her, and his firm but gentle hand curled around her arm. It was a reminder that she had to stay.

Like she needed one.

Chapter Nine

Jose

When Carlos returned, I was cowering in the corner, face down and shivering. Though the killer had gone away, I feared he would come back. What of all the other murderers and cutthroats? We weren't even safe from the *polícia*. I had no one to turn to, nowhere to go. Silent tears streaked my face, but the fear of being overheard stopped me from sobbing like a girl.

"Pedro?" Carlos' voice was hesitant. "Are you okay? Did you see it?"

I nodded.

"Do you want to talk?"

I shook my head.

"Would you rather be alone?"

"No, don't go, please," I pleaded.

Without another word he sat down close beside me.

The sound of a siren drew nearer. A common noise overheard a lot on the streets, but I hadn't heard them come this close. Thoughts of the drive by shootings flashed through my head. What had once seemed incomprehensible, now lay within the realms of my imagination.

"Should we run?" Panic flashed like a neon sign in my words.

"No need. They are not here for us. They don't advertise their presence for a shoot-out. They have come for the body. If they ask you if you saw anything, you say you were asleep."

"Could I get into trouble?"

"Only if the killer knows you witnessed it."

The *policía* didn't come over to ask. According to Carlos, they didn't care.

"He was a nobody. It would have been different if he was rich, influential, or a tourist. Someone who mattered."

I felt the stirrings of rage. *Someone who mattered?* How had God allowed some people to be classified as important while others did not matter?

"I'll go and get us some food," Carlos said once the *policía* had left and everything had settled back to normal. Or, as normal as it got here.

I wanted to go with him but knew I should not be seen out when I was supposed to be ill.

As the days passed, I wondered how many more I would have to endure. Chico visited daily, reporting that Martinez was becoming less tolerant of my illness, which seemed to be getting worse. After each coughing attack I was left feeling weaker. Carlos was a welcome visitor, and as the days passed, we got to know each other better. I now thought of him as my best friend—well, after Pedro, of course.

An assiduous thought slid into my head. I tried to dismiss it. My brother would never betray me. *Maybe he won't be able to help himself.* The life he was glimpsing now

146

could be too strong of a temptation for his own self-control. Was it his turn for that life, and mine for this one?

"How do you get used to living like this, Carlos?"

"It isn't a choice. No one says to you, 'Would you like this life?' You cope with it, and you do that because it's do or die. So, maybe there is a choice, but while there is even the smallest chance that one day there will be an escape, then I have to keep going on. You get to see those who no longer have hope and it seems to me that it is a living death—far worse than death itself."

We fell silent, which had become our habit when Carlos regaled me with these rare long speeches.

"Do you think Pedro will be much longer?" Carlos broke the silence.

"I don't know, Carlos. I have such mixed feelings. I want to go back to my old life. But now that I know about Pedro, I don't think things can ever be the same. How can I live that life when I know what he endures?" I paused. "What you endure, too."

Carlos said nothing. Once I would have taken that as a sign of him being simple, but now I knew he was processing the information, and the reason he didn't respond was because there was no answer. He didn't use words just for the sake of them.

I had often complained to my parents of being bored. It was almost laughable now. The tedium of living on the streets was beyond anything my mind could have comprehended.

"Could you teach me some Eengleesh?" Carlos asked out of the blue.

"English. Yes, I can, but first you must say the word correctly."

"Engleesh."

I laughed, a gentle teasing sound meant to break the tension Carlos felt without belittling him.

"It's hard."

"So was learning Portuguese for me."

"You are perfect, fluent."

"My parents made me attend lessons every Sunday, then Father would test me afterward to make sure I had learnt something new. He would also set me tasks to do in the week. *Mamãe* started to coach me. With her it was easy and fun. Father is more intense."

"Okay."

"Try in."

"In?" His dark brows drew together.

"Glish."

"Glish."

"Okay put that together."

"Inglish."

"In…glish. Inglish."

"That's great. Carlos, when you go for food later, can you pick up a pencil and paper from the money my parents gave us?" I handed him a coin from my small collection. "I will also teach you to read and write the words you will learn." It felt exciting to have this new challenge. Shame it could be for such a short time.

"Are you hungry? I could go now?" Carlos' eagerness to learn was infectious.

He arrived back with a patty for each of us which he told me was *Acaraje* and *Pào de quijo*—cheese and bread. He also produced a pencil and a small pad of paper, and then handed me some coins, my change. We savoured the food but were both eager to get on with a different task.

"I have never craved something more than food." He laughed.

I took the pad and wrote the word 'English' at the top. I did not use joined up writing, but spaced the letters so that Carlos would be able to read them. I handed him the pencil, which he held stiffly at first.

Then it seemed his memory flooded back as, in a neat script, he copied the word.

"*Bom dia,*" I said.

"It isn't *dia.*"

"Good morning."

Carlos' brows drew together again but then they relaxed back into place and the lines that had formed on his forehead disappeared.

"Goo…" he stopped.

"Good."

"Good," He copied.

I nodded. "Morning."

"More… ning."

"Good morning."

"Good morning." I clapped as though he were a small child, and we both fell backwards laughing.

"You must be better if you can laugh like that." I didn't recognise the voice but the tall *policial* whose shirt was stretched over his taut belly, and who had hard, flint eyes could only be Martinez.

"Not exactly, Detective Inspector, but sometimes you have to laugh."

"I see that Chico is correct, little Carlos is now your constant companion. Some boys like that kind of thing. I didn't realise you were like that, Pedro, but it could be a very good earner."

I started to cough and could see the fear on Carlos' face as he pressed himself against the wall to make himself as inconspicuous as possible. The coughing continued; my throat was now raw.

"Get him a drink," Martinez commanded of the other officer beside him.

I gulped the drink down and then lay back, exhausted.

"If you don't get better soon, you won't be of any use to me."

The implied threat was clear, and I now understood what I had perceived before as kindness, to be anything but. Carlos still melded into the wall long after the *policía* had gone.

"Carlos, what's wrong?" His body was rigid now. Our joyfulness of earlier had fled.

His sobs could be heard before his tears were visible, but soon they splattered unheeding down his cheeks and over his ragged shirt.

"Tell me what's wrong, Carlos? Did Martinez say something—do something?" I probed, and he shook his head.

"Was it the other *policía*?" His wild, dilated eyes told me I was right, so I pressed, "Did he do something to you?"

He bowed his head.

"Did he hurt you? Beat you?"

It took an age before Carlos spoke. The confident boy I'd started to get to know had reverted back to the boy I'd first met, the one who stuttered and struggled to form his words.

"I… it happened three years ago, but I remember it like it was yesterday. It haunts me still." He paused and for a moment I thought that he wasn't going to say anything else. "The *policial*, he asked me if I would work for him, serve food and drink to him and his friends. They were playing cards for money, poker they called it. The room was dark and dirty, and filled with the smoke of their cigarettes and cigars. I brought out platters of food that made my mouth water and hoped that they would let me take the leftovers in addition to the coins he gave me. I had to pour their drinks and they were all pretty drunk by the end of the evening." Carlos' face revealed fear and horror as he continued his tale.

"One of the men pinched my cheek and said that I was cute. The *policial*, he told the man that for a fee he… could have me…"

I frowned not understanding what he meant.

"I tried to run… truly I did. Hands clamped onto my arms, nails biting into my skin. He reeked of alcohol, tobacco, and body odour. I thought I was going to get sick. I struggled, but he was strong."

Nausea built up in me as Carlos continued his story and realisation dawned on me what he meant.

"'You've done this before, haven't you?' the policial asked me. I thought he would let me go when I said no, but he

didn't." A sob escaped. "*'I'll take first shot, it's a rarity to get an innocent for the plucking.'* I pleaded with him to stop but he wouldn't. His friends held me down as he… as he raped me… and then they took their turns."

I reached out and held his shaking body while he rocked back and forth bawling his eyes out.

Pedro

It was the third night before I slept through with both eyes closed and was able to understand what a luxury it was. The first morning it had taken all my willpower to rise from the bed. Even the bed I had shared with DC and Jonny had not been this soft. And the pillows—I couldn't find adequate words to describe them. It was on that first day though that I also discovered the pleasures and excitement to be had from new clothes and three meals a day laid out before me. I didn't have to beg or steal. The only thing I did have to do for our evening meal, was go down to the restaurant. The first time had been daunting. If I'd thought the cutlery was confusing when we'd eaten in the suite, that was nothing compared to the white linen-clad tables with their confusing array of sparkling cutlery and glasses.

I bounded out of bed, eager to see what today would bring. Pattering on silent feet through the rooms—Fernando would berate me for not wearing shoes—felt so good. When I heard them speaking in their bedroom, I hesitated. There was an urgency in the quiet way they spoke. I should've just walked on, but something in the way they were speaking caused me to pause and press an ear to the cold wooden door.

"I am worried by how skinny he has become. He was only on the streets a couple of days."

"His cough seems to have improved, though," Fernando answered.

"That is the least of his problems. I think we should visit the hospital for a check-up."

I waited for Fernando to dismiss her fears as being overprotective.

"That's not such a bad idea. We'll see what the private detective has discovered about his brother, too."

After padding back to my room I knew Jose had been right. I'd thought he'd suffered from an over fertile imagination, but now I, too, had heard their plan. There was something nagging away in the furthest recesses of my brain. Throwing myself back onto the bed I buried myself beneath the covers.

If they think I'm skinny and need to see a doctor, they should see the other kids on the street, I thought. An image of Jonny before he was killed flashed into my mind. I tried not to consider Jose and how he was faring. It seemed easier somehow not to.

After ten minutes, I got up again and put on the shoes I hated so much so that this time, when I walked down the corridor, they would hear my steps.

Christina opened the bedroom door and swept me into her arms.

Clinging to her, I inhaled the sweet smell of her perfume. This life could be easy to get used to, and I had to quell all thoughts about having to give this up. Maybe there was a way I could stay after all. *He's had this life for years, maybe now it is my turn.*

"No!"

I realised by the shocked way Christina turned to me that I had voiced this out loud. All I had wanted to do was silence the internal battle.

"What is it, Jose?"

The love she felt for me—no, not for me, for Jose, was apparent. I pulled away from her gentle touch.

"What is it, Jose? You can tell your *mamãe* anything."

Though I longed to tell her, I didn't want to see the rejection when she realised I wasn't Jose—and yet, hadn't she sought me out anyway? So, maybe she would be pleased, and then… and then… but I couldn't go on.

"Nothing's wrong, *Mamãe*."

Her brows knitted together. "Your Father and I think we should make an appointment at the hospital, Jose. To check out your cough."

"But it's gone now." I hoped it was true; a fleeting memory of Jose coughing and how weak he had looked afterward flashed into my mind.

"Well, it never hurts to be checked out, *bebê*."

After breakfast—a feast of scrambled eggs with sausage and bacon on toast—I excused myself and went back to my room. Something didn't add up. It had occurred to me before, but now it plagued me. This obsession with Jose's health was strange. Was there something he hadn't told me? Maybe it was something they hadn't told him. In that moment, the luxury which had turned my head fled while a small thread of fear wove around my heart. The urge to run out of the hotel and find him and see if he was okay was strong, but I knew I wouldn't be allowed out. Although they never said anything, I could feel their eyes watching my every move and felt sure that the hotel staff wouldn't allow me to leave either. It made me realise my brother was much more resourceful than I'd given him credit for. But if he weren't well, that didn't explain them wanting to replace Jose with me... *does it? Did the desire to replace him come because he is ill?* The idea, so cold, and calculating worthy of Martinez, made me heave. I rushed from my room to the bathroom where I emptied the contents of my stomach.

Cool hands rubbed my back and I looked up to see Christina's tear-filled eyes. Fernando stood over us with a face cloth which he handed to Christina after running it under the cold tap. The look on his face made me gasp.

"What is it? What aren't you telling me?"

Fernando gave Christina a warning look; she was to say nothing. So, instead of an answer, she wiped my face with the cool cloth and then placed a tender kiss on my head. Fernando reached down and positioned one hand under my knees and the other behind my back. He scooped me up and carried me back to my room.

"Rest here, *meu filho*."

The gentle timbre of his voice scared me more than anything. He wasn't planning on giving me—Jose—away. Fernando's love was etched throughout the worry lines marking his face. His eyes were clouded and a tear sat in the corner. He wiped it away with the back of his hand before stalking from the room. It appeared as though anger dictated his steps but I realised it was fear.

"*Mamãe?*" I pleaded.

"Rest, *Filho*."

"I feel fine. Why should I rest?"

"Please, Jose. Please just do as we ask of you." Tears rolled down her face, and she neither tried to hide them nor wipe them away.

"Please," I tried again while she sat on my bed and stroked my hair. I threw my arms around her waist and sobbed, not really knowing why. Perhaps what *wasn't* being said disturbed me more?

After a while she rose and left the room, closing the door behind her. My tears had stopped but my head hurt from trying to figure out all the pieces. I longed to talk to Jose. More than anything I wanted to talk to DC—he would have made sense of it all. More tears burnt a path down my cheeks. Now that they had started, they weren't inclined to stop. I cried tears for everything. For Jonny, for DC, for Jose and myself. For the lives we endured. No one ever said life would be easy, but surely it shouldn't be so hard? Why did some people have it all and yet others had it so tough? But then, when one looked closely, *did* they have it all? I would have said Jose, Fernando, and Christina had it all, but they hid something. Their tears were proof not everything was as it seemed. What were they hiding? Releasing the pillow

I'd muffled my sobs with I lay there, still, looking up at the ceiling. It was a strange feeling to look up and not see the sky.

One of the drawers in the bedside cabinet held Jose's books. I had been reading *The Hobbit* since my first night here. Some of the words were beyond my comprehension, but the escapism that I found as soon as I opened the pages was enjoyable. The descriptions of the wizard and Bilbo, who was happy with his life until Gandalf came along and uprooted him from his cosy existence to bring adventure where it wasn't wanted, made me laugh.

I touched the book with every intention of picking it up but something stayed my hand. With my heart beating at what felt like twice the normal pace, I delved down deeper and removed the paper parcel which had once belonged to DC. I had never considered opening it before, but now something drew me, an invisible force. If I'd believed in ghosts, I might've thought it was DC himself. I shivered. With fingers that shook, I released the twine binding an expensive-looking leather journal. It must have been something from his time before he lived on the streets. He hadn't told me much, little snippets, but nothing personal. The word on the streets was that he used to be a lawyer.

Lifting the journal with both hands, I stroked the soft brown leather with a reverence others reserved for holy relics. I raised it to my face and breathed in the faint smell of leather, noting the even less distinct smell of DC as I hugged it to me. It was a precious reminder of the man who had become the only father I had known.

A dirtied ribbon that might once have born a resemblance to the colour red was tied together in a neat bow, holding the pages together along the unbound side. Pulling at one length, the bow disappeared, as though it had never been, leaving a loose single knot. Sliding my finger beneath, I separated them until they both lay at opposite ends, trailing limply. I pushed the hard cover over, and then, with a mist of tears in my eyes, read the words inside:

This journal is the property of Daniel Cortez latterly known as DC. I declare myself to be of sound mind and body, though many on the streets may not concur. Inside these pages I will give a true and unbiased account of what led me here. These are not the ramblings of an egotistical man wanting to leave his mark on the world, but the desire of said man to leave behind the truth so that future generations will know what I could not tell at the time—and may not get a chance to tell in my lifetime. My only hope is that this journal stays intact and doesn't fall into the wrong hands, where it would be dangerous.

When the words on this page came to a stop, I paused. *Daniel Cortez,* I played with this name on my tongue. A ball of fear lodged in my stomach, underneath my ribcage. By opening the next pages, I would read something I'd be unable to erase from my memory. DC hadn't been prone to exaggeration. The enormity of this burden of responsibility pressed down on my shoulders. After a few deep breaths I turned over the thick cream sheet of paper.

I owed it to DC.

The Exiles – England

Carolina

Carolina felt her brain whirling, going around in circles like an overhead fan. She played Leandro's words over in her head, including the things he'd left unsaid. Just because she had episodes where life and her memories became overwhelming, didn't mean she wasn't able to piece together what was happening here and now.

It was imperative that she got out of here in time for the trip back home to Brasil. Leandro would argue that she wasn't well enough, so, she had to prove to him that she was. Carolina knew once they placed her babies back in her arms, all would be well.

Chapter Ten

Jose

As the days passed, my panic grew. I wanted to keep faith in Pedro, but the continual lack of word from him seemed ominous. The logical part of my brain told me the decision was not in his hands, though. When my parents decided that it was time to swap, they would. A snatch of conversation came back to me. *Of course!* They were waiting for the private investigator to find me. If we'd thought about it more, we could have arranged for Carlos to let slip about knowing someone who was the spitting image. I knew my brother cared for me, but I couldn't help considering how he would come back to this life after tasting mine. What if he'd already told them who he was so there would be no need to swap?

Carlos had been distant since his confession, as though he were ashamed. I wanted to broach the subject, but didn't know what to say. It wasn't his fault; I didn't view him any differently, but the words which formed in my head would not make their way to my mouth.

"What will I do if Martinez makes me go out stealing? I would be caught straight away."

"Pedro will be back soon. No point in worrying about what isn't going to happen."

His words did nothing to reassure me, but whingeing like a girl wouldn't get me anywhere.

"Jose, do you think we could start up those English lessons again?"

In the aftermath of the visit by the *policía,* and the revelation of abuse from Carlos, we had forgotten. Well, put it aside.

"Yes, Carlos. Nice pronunciation of English by the way."

A shy smile lit up his face. I spent hours talking and writing, with Carlos copying me. I won't pretend that he was a natural, but he did pick it up after a few attempts. For the time being, I was only teaching him words. After a while I decided to try to get him to string a sentence together. I told him to copy me, but to change his name.

"Hello, my name is Jose."

"Heylo, my name eez Carlos."

I smiled, and he did too. It was the first time I had seen his elfin face light up since that night.

"I know you must go, Jose, but I don't want you to."

He wasn't expecting an answer and I had nothing to say. I knew I couldn't survive the streets. Maybe if I'd been exposed to them as Pedro had from the beginning, but not now. I didn't want to lose the bond I had with Carlos either. I'd always struggled with friendships in England, not being the typical boy who loved football and fighting like the other boys in my class. Pedro and Carlos were the first boys who had accepted me for who I was, and I didn't want to lose them.

After Carlos left, I lay back on my bed. I hadn't wanted to worry him, but I wasn't feeling at all well. Light-headed, I fought for breath. My stomach knotted. I was alone, and knew this wasn't the result of a silly chest infection. The night dragged by slower than any I'd ever known. Every second felt like an hour. My breathing rasped with the regularity of the *tick-tock* of a clock. My life hung in the balance, and as a street urchin, no one would care.

The first light of dawn spread its fingers across the sky. From my position, I watched the red ball rise on the horizon while the sky lit up with a pastel rainbow palate.

"Jose," Carlos hissed. "I couldn't wait any longer. I've been practising and—" His words cut off when he looked at me.

I couldn't move. I had no strength left and was sure the colour had fled my face. Looking up at him with eyes that felt dull and lifeless, I managed to croak out, "Help me."

Horrified, I watched as he ran off. His fear had just condemned me to death.

Pedro

The biggest discovery of all time was discovered by Leandro and myself. We had been part of a research team tasked with finding renewable energy. Leandro and I were top of our field, but we were also part of a team of seven men. So, while Leandro and I made the ultimate discovery, we had worked as part of a unit. Teo, Leandro, and I studied together at University. We had called ourselves 'The Hit Squad.' We were young and idealistic, and thought the world was ours for the taking. "We will rule the world," Teo would claim with all the insolence of youth. Leandro would laugh at his friend's confidence, for while he didn't agree with that sentiment, he knew we had the potential to come up with innovatory ideas. Science wasn't the boring subject at school that so many believed it to be. For us, it was our passion. We ate, slept, and breathed it. Girls didn't even play a part of our lives, until Leandro fell in love with the graceful, exquisite Carolina. I think we were all a little bit in love with her. She wore elegance in that way someone with good breeding has. I could not hate Leandro even though I knew I would never meet a woman who would compare. Don't get me wrong, I had my fair share of women, but none of them had my heart. Leandro was the brother I never had, the other half of my soul. I would have died for him. Teo joined us but he was never one of us... well, not in the same way.

I stopped reading at the sound of voices raised in anger. Tucking the journal into my waistband, I tiptoed to the door so I could hear better.

"We can't lie to him anymore."

"We can't tell him the truth."

"He will find out sooner or later, Fernando. We should tell him."

"Oh. Jose, you have a twin brother. We adopted you but not him..." I almost walked away since I knew it all already,

170

but his next words halted me mid-step, *"...we have to find him now, as he may be the only one who can save your life."*

Two broken sobs came from the bedroom, and I stood stock still, unable to move even had I wanted.

"No!" The scream tore at my throat, ripping at my vocal chords.

The bedroom door flew open. Fernando and Christina stood there with shocked expressions and tears streaming down their cheeks.

"Jose, I am so sorry. I didn't want you to find out like that."

I screamed again, broken sobs choking me so that my breaths came in gasps.

"Oh *Deus*, Fernando! Call an ambulance!" Christina cried.

"No!" I shouted, stopping them. "Jose," I rasped, and they looked at me as though I had lost all semblance of sanity. "We have to get him. He can't be out there if he's ill."

A sharp rapping on the door distracted us. Fernando walked to the door without wiping the evidence of his distress from his face. In the doorway stood the hotel manager, his shoulders were drooped and he wore an expression of apology.

"*Senhor* Sanchez, I apologise for the intrusion."

"What is it?"

"A…" his nose winked in distaste, "…street urchin, the one who brought your son back, claims he has your son. The boy was most insistent saying your son was ill. But I can see he is with you. The little brat clearly wants more money."

"Wait," I shouted as Fernando started to dismiss him. "That's Carlos, you have to listen to him. Jose must be bad for Carlos to have come here." Seeing their shocked expression, I added hastily, "I'm the twin you're looking for… I will explain later. You *must* listen to Carlos. Jose is in danger."

I think my tone of voice rather than my words echoed in Christina's head, as she lost her colour. I grabbed her hand and together we ran for the lift. Fernando and the manager followed.

"Carlos," I panted as we exited the revolving doors.

"Pedro, come quick. I think Jose is dying."

"Follow me," I commanded. I knew the back streets better than Carlos.

A thundering of feet rumbled behind me as Fernando, Christina, and Carlos followed. Although I wasn't trying to outrun anyone, my feet moved as though they were guided by angel wings.

"Jose!" I cried, and threw myself into the doorway which had been my home as Christina screamed for help.

A shopkeeper heard her and called the emergency services. Soon, the _ambulância_ and _polícia_ arrived together. Martinez stepped from the car and looked from me to Jose, who was now placed on a stretcher. His eyes widened in what I assumed to be confusion, but my troubled brain could not comprehend more beyond the fact that my brother was seriously ill.

"Christina, you go with Jose in the ambulance and I will bring…"

"Pedro," I supplied, then added in a pleading tone "And Carlos too?"

He seemed to consider it, and then nodded. "But I want answers young man."

"I will tell you everything when I see Jose safely in the hands of the doctors." I expected him to argue, but he didn't.

Martinez stepped between us. "Come with me, Pedro."

Drawing himself up to his full impressive height, Fernando pushed his way between Martinez and me, and then utilised a tone of voice that clearly said he was used to being obeyed. "What is the problem, Detective Inspector? This young man is with me. What business do you have with him?"

I couldn't keep the satisfied look out of my eyes witnessing someone getting the upper hand on the detective. His eyes narrowed, a promise of the vengeance he wanted to exact, but this moment would be etched on my brain for the rest of my life—no matter how short.

"Apologies, *Senhor*. I thought this boy was bothering you."

"Despicable cretin," Fernando said after ushering Carlos and me into the taxi, where Carlos' peals of laughter joined mine.

"I've never heard you laugh before, Carlos," I said when our gaiety died down.

"I never had reason before. Jose made me laugh. Jose was teaching me English." His tongue stumbled over the word as silent tears ran down his cheeks. I gathered him in my arms while noticing the look Fernando gave us from the passenger seat.

The Exiles – England

Carolina

"Your wife seems to have made a quick recovery this time."

"Seems to have?" Leandro questioned.

"She has. She's done remarkably well."

Carolina's calm, beatific smile hid her chaotic thoughts that were spiralling vortex-like, in her head while she played up to the doctor and her husband. It had been simple, really. All they wanted was for her to acknowledge that she'd had a psychotic episode, and then verbalise in a calm manner that she was feeling herself again and could recognise the triggers. It had taken a little bit of searching through the dusty corners of her brain, swishing away the cobwebs, to remember what had worked previously. Before, it had been an organic process. This time it had been a manipulation.

"Leandro, dear, I'm sorry that I put you through that again." She turned her warm, caramel eyes on him, locking them on his. She didn't want to overplay her hand, though; she didn't want to make him suspicious. Her words did have a ring of truth to them. Carolina loved her husband and didn't like causing him distress.

His fingers splayed on her knees, giving it a tiny squeeze. There was a time when this would have precipitated a passionate embrace, but now, it was a symbol of his support. Her eyes glazed over at the memory of sweeter times.

"Caro? What is it?" Leandro asked.

"A memory of happier times, my darling. Nothing to worry about." The open gaze she gave him must have worked as he looked relieved.

"Just sign the release papers, Leandro, and you can take your wife home."

With a flourish, her husband signed her out as Leandro Cordosa, the name he'd assumed when he'd fled Brasil, the name that was on his passport. She knew he now signed as Mister, not Professor. The loss of his name had stripped him of his identity in every way. Mr. Leandro Cordosa was a taxi driver. Leandro polished his cab every day, though; he believed in taking pride in his work even if it wasn't the job he had trained hard for.

Leandro

Leandro had always been the studious one while his brother raised hell in the bars and clubs. He used the family name to get his position; hard work had never been on his agenda. Even as a young boy, Paolo had torn the wings off flies and revelled in ensnaring animals then watching with amusement as they struggled in vain against the deadly teeth of the trap. Leandro had never used these tools when he had gone hunting with their father. The bullet was quicker, and less cruel, on the animal. They only hunted for food, not pleasure.

"There is less waste when you use a trap," Paolo would protest. *"You have to cut away the area where the bullet enters."*

"It is more humane, Paolo. The animal doesn't suffer as it is over quickly."

"Who cares about the animal?" He'd scoff.

It was thanks to Paolo's lack of marksmanship that Leandro and Carolina owed their lives. Leandro knew that had *he* been the one with the gun, he would have aimed at, and hit, a vital organ. However, killing his fellow man had never appealed to Leandro.

Psychiatrist

"Mr Cordosa, Leandro?"

Leandro looked up into the cerulean eyes of the psychiatrist. "It was my turn to think about the past."

"Not happy memories would be my guess."

"No, not happy memories."

"You really should tell me everything."

Of course, he knew they wouldn't. Every six months to a year, Carolina would come in, but they refused to tell him the darkest secrets eating away at their souls. He shuddered to imagine what the couple had endured; the scars in their eyes and heart, in addition to the visible ones on their bodies, were evidence of something awful. He'd almost given up berating them, knowing that he was, in essence, treating her emotional and psychological wounds with the equivalent of a plaster. If he could only get to the bottom of their story, he was sure he could start to rebuild Carolina. He always ended these sessions with a half-hearted yet genuine attempt to get them to open up.

Chapter Eleven

Jose

I heard the anguished cry of my name moments before Pedro threw himself down beside me. *He came back*, I thought. I think I said his name, although I don't remember anything else after that.

The next thing I knew, I was waking up in a hospital bed with a tube coming out of my nose, along with one from my arm. Disorientated, I looked around and saw *Mamãe* asleep in a hard-looking chair. *What happened?* The last thing I remembered was feeling ill and seeing Carlos run off. *Was all of that a dream? Did Pedro exist?*

"*Mamãe*," I whispered the word, halfway between not wanting to wake her up, and needing her at the same time.

She shot off the chair, eyes wide and full of tenderness. "*Meu bebê, meu filho, meu coração.*" Covering my face with kisses, she fretted over me. "Stay still, my love, you've had us worried. You were—you *are* very ill. We should have told you before. Pedro is outside with your father."

"He is? He told you everything?"

"No, we said we would wait for explanations until you came around. He is dying to see you. I have never seen someone run so fast as he did when Carlos told him you were ill."

"Carlos?"

"He is here. Father arranged for him to have a bath and a proper meal. He sent out for some clothes for him, too. We owe him your life."

"What is wrong with me, *Mamãe*?"

"If you can wait a few more minutes we will tell you everything, with Pedro. Then we only have to say it once, okay?"

I didn't have to wait long before Father, Pedro, and a smartly-dressed boy, clean from head to toe, cautiously entered the room.

"Come in, come in," *Mamãe* said, then added, "But we don't want to tire him out."

I smiled a welcome, and was struck by the tears in Father's eyes.

He came to my bedside, opposite *Mamãe,* and kissed my head. "Now someone speak," he growled as he walked around the bed to stand at *Mamãe's* shoulder where he rested his hand on it.

Pedro came and lay beside me on the bed, leaving the chair for Carlos. I didn't miss the look in my parents' eyes when Pedro touched his head to mine.

"I will tell the story as Jose isn't up to speaking." He paused a long time, as though wondering where to start, and then began. "Jose found me on the streets after leaving the hotel. Some acquaintances of mine thought Jose was me, and when Jose told them who he was, they thought they could make money by bringing him to me. I won't tell you everything, but he told me that he'd overheard you talking. He heard you say he was adopted, that he had a twin, and that you wanted a private detective to find me."

Mamãe let out a sob as Father squeezed her shoulder. "Why didn't you both come back, then?"

"Jose thought… you, *Senhor*, especially, were not proud of him, and that you wanted to swap him."

They both gasped.

"Why would you think that?" *Mamãe* looked straight at me and clutched my hand, bringing it to her heart. "We love you more than life. You are our *filho*."

Tears welled up in my eyes.

"He heard you say that she had made the wrong choice," Pedro addressed Father. "A long time ago."

They both kept silent while the memory of that argument came back to them.

"*Filho*, that is the senseless kind of thing adults say when angry. You had made me cross that day, but I would never lose you. I don't say it, *Filho*, and *Mamãe* tells me I am too tough on you, but I do love you."

After I wiped my tears away, Pedro continued, "It was my idea to swap places. I figured if you were going to take me in, I'd pretend to be Jose, so that when you

184

made the swap, I would be back on the streets, and Jose would be safe with you."

Pedro looked at me and then said in an undertone, "I struggled, Jose. Being fed three times a day without having to steal or scavenge in bins. The clean clothes and a bed. I think the best part was when I realised I didn't need to sleep with one eye open. I wouldn't have left you out there—no matter how hard it would have been to leave this. Sorry."

His honesty was one of the things which made my twin so very special.

"That is why you got so angry about our food waste," Father said to Pedro, his expression asking for forgiveness for something I knew nothing about.

"Enough," I rasped then looked at Pedro, willing him to know what I wanted to say. As my twin, even that one word was enough.

"Jose wants… no, *we* want the truth from you," Pedro said.

A doctor in a white coat entered the room, looked at my charts, and said, "I think this young man has had enough. You must let him rest."

Mamãe half-lifted from her chair, but Pedro stopped her.

"No, Jose must know now. He can't handle not knowing."

"Okay, Jose." Father took a deep breath. "You have a problem with your kidneys. When you went in for that persistent cough and they ran all those tests on you, that's when they discovered it. We were going to start you on dialysis when you got home. The doctor said we had a small window before we needed to start it, but ultimately he thought you would need a transplant. We were tested and not found to be a match…" He stopped and looked with a sheepish expression at Pedro.

"You just wanted to find me to be a donor?" I could hear the anger in Pedro's voice, and his body shook alongside me. "You didn't want me as a baby, but you wanted to find me to take part of my body? What then? Shove me back onto the streets once my usefulness to you was finished?"

I held his hand, mindful of his pain, knowing his anger was not aimed at me.

"Not now, Pedro," Father warned. "I will take your wrath, but I do not want my son, *your brother*, to be distressed by this while he is ill. Take it out on me, and only me, later."

"Why only you? Why not Christina, too?" Pedro's words were a fraction above a whisper.

I looked askance at them, I also wanted to know.

With reluctance, Father explained how *Mamãe* had wanted us both, but he had made her choose because he didn't think she was strong enough to cope with twins.

"Why me?" I rasped. The doctor clicked his teeth in disapproval, but I ignored him and stared straight at *Mamãe,* waiting for her answer.

"I wanted you both. I did. When I put my hands into the cot, to you both, Jose clasped my finger. It was like he had chosen me. He seemed to need me more. Pedro, you let out a cry, but you seemed... I don't know... stronger. I'm sorry." Tears ran down her cheeks.

Pedro

It was with great reluctance that I left Jose in the hands of the doctor. His pallor frightened me. Before I left, I wrapped my arms around him and whispered, "You can have my kidney, Jose. I can't lose you, too."

A watery smile stretched his lips but I could tell even that effort drained him. A lump lodged in my throat while I walked away, head bowed.

The doctor insisted everyone should leave afterward. Jose needed rest now, with no more emotional upheaval. I could hear the condemnation in the words he'd left unsaid. Jose had been too weak for what had happened, but at the same time he needed to know the truth sooner rather than later. A wild imagination can be worse than reality.

We were led back across the hall by a nurse in a starched white uniform with a stern expression. "You can wait here."

"I'm sorry, Pedro," Fernando broke the silence.

Carlos was cowering in the corner. He hated loud voices or confrontation.

I didn't reply to Fernando. I couldn't be sure that I wouldn't scream at him the way my insides churned, so I said nothing. He was determined to get a response, though; maybe he wanted forgiveness, atonement for his sins. For that he should have gone to a priest, not a boy who he'd condemned to the mercies of the streets.

"I know you live on the streets now, Pedro, but you must have had a different life once, a better one? You are well-educated, and your command of the English language is flawless. You don't get that on the streets." He was seeking to forgive himself, since I would not offer mine.

"Oh, really?" I spat the words out. My hands trembled and a painful knot tied up my insides. "I was thrown out of the orphanage at the tender age of one. I was no longer at the age where a childless couple would buy me. I was thrown into an *aléia,* along with the trash and another boy. I was picked up by a man who I came to know as DC." There was no point mentioning that I knew his real name now. "He took me in with the other boy. We lived on the streets. He gave me my name, and the other boy he named Jonny. He gave us an education and taught us how to survive the streets." I couldn't continue as memories mingled with my anger.

No one said anything while they waited for me to continue. Carlos was shivering now.

"That *policial* who tried to stop me from coming with you today, sim, you remember him?"

Fernando nodded.

"His name is Martinez, Detective Inspector Martinez." The words tasted like poison on my lips. "He is the most corrupt officer on a force renowned for corruption. He arranges all the petty crime, and then takes the largest cut. He also arranges the drive-by shootings."

Christina's hands flew to her mouth as she tried to hold back her shock.

"Shootings?" Fernando looked at me. His brown eyes met mine, as though reaching into my soul to determine a truth he couldn't comprehend.

"There are too many *pivethinos* on the streets. We're seen as human rats. Tourists don't like to see us, so they cull the numbers for their sake. The *polícia* spray bullets into us. Well, not me or Carlos—not yet. I managed to get away last time. I would have been dead if it hadn't been for DC, though. I was hiding behind a car when they gunned him down, and Jonny, too. I watched them die."

Fernando's eyes popped wide and his face turned ashen. He covered his face, and his head fell between his knees as though it were too heavy to be held up by his neck. His shoulders shook with the sobs that wracked his body.

When I looked at Christina, silent tears streaked her face. Christina stood up and gathered me into her arms. She motioned to Carlos, too, and soon we were all in one embrace, crying.

Fernando sat outside the circle; he did not try to join us. His eyes were reddened and scarred by the horror I'd described. In that moment, my anger now spent, I couldn't help but pity him. Although he had made his wife choose, he had not set out to reject me. It hadn't been personal. A man from a different world, he couldn't have understood how it worked, and so, he had given his love to Jose. If they hadn't taken Jose that day, my brother could've been killed with DC and Jonny. The streets had taught me to be tough, but DC had countered those lessons by teaching me to be fair.

Pulling away from Carlos and Christina, I walked the few steps to Fernando, whose head still hung between his legs. I wrapped my arms around his shoulders. Haggard, he looked up at me before pushing his head into my stomach and wrapping his arms around me.

"I promise to never let any harm come to you again," he vowed.

"And Carlos, too," Christina added. Her words held a note of authority that I was sure Fernando had never heard before.

Carlos snuggled deeper into her warm embrace.

"And Carlos, too." Fernando repeated.

I watched Carlos' shoulders droop, and it dawned on me that I'd never seen him relaxed before. "I will be the donor for Jose," I said after a moment.

We'd been sitting in silence, letting our emotions come back under control.

"Are you sure? We still want you to be part of the family, even if you decide that's too much." Christina lay a hand on mine.

"He's my brother."

"They will need to test you to see whether you are a match, and then they will talk to you about what is involved if you are. Just remember you can say no at any point."

"We can't all hang around the hospital cluttering it up," Fernando declared. "I'll take the boys back to the hotel. I should start looking at getting a solicitor so we can adopt Pedro and Carlos as soon as possible."

We popped our heads around the door to say goodbye to Jose, but he was fast asleep.

"Tell him we're all going to be one family, won't you, Christina?"

"You can call me *Mamãe* if you want."

I stayed silent. I wasn't sure I was ready to do that. It was all coming at once, there was too much to take in.

"When you're ready." Her smile was gentle.

Fernando placed one hand on the small of my back and the other on Carlos, who immediately shied away. We were outside the room now.

"What is it, Carlos? I won't hurt you."

Carlos said nothing.

"For now you can share with Pedro, in Jose's room."

Carlos nodded, the excitement from earlier leaving him as he looked around. His face should've been filled with awe at his new surroundings, but he appeared to be searching for an escape route.

"What is it, Carlos?" I asked.

His lips were clamped shut, mute.

"Carlos, if we are to be a family, we can't have any secrets. We tried that before, and look what happened," Fernando said.

Haltingly, he told his story—about his parents and their death, then being rejected by his uncle and the multiple rapes he had endured. Hairs rose on my arms hearing the horror of his tale. We had all suffered on the streets, but this was beyond comprehension. Even as I thought it, my mind wandered to the rent boys, not all of whom had chosen to make a living that way.

Fernando made the same promise to Carlos and me. No one would ever hurt us again nor would he ever allow a man to touch us. "You have nothing to fear from me... except maybe my stern demeanour." His laugh eased the mood. "But I promise I will work on that."

I won't say that Carlos threw himself headlong into his new parent's arms, but he did relax again.

The Exiles – England

Leandro

The new passports arrived in the name of Leandro and Carolina Cordosa. Having been British citizens for these past two years had made it a lot easier. Leandro had argued and pleaded with his wife. For every objection he put forward, she countered with a reasonable explanation, until he couldn't find any more excuses. His gut told him he was wrong, but he was a learned man who believed more in the head than the flimsiness of a gut reaction.

"If we find out that our boys… are no longer alive?" he tried one last tactic knowing it to be a low blow, and not one he was comfortable using. However, it was also a distinct possibility.

Carolina

"It will put an end to the not knowing and allow me to grieve in the normal way," Carolina kept her voice steady as she spoke despite a whole host of butterflies battering inside her chest. She feared that she was experiencing the beginning of a heart attack. Her serene countenance fooled Leandro. The long, deep breaths that the therapist had taught her—in through the nose, out through the mouth—steadied the flapping in her chest. More panic than heart attack. She almost laughed out loud but realised this would make her seem crazy.

"Do you remember the last time we were on an airplane?"

He seemed determined to make her crack. She knew he was trying to see how far he could push her. If she snapped now, he would fly to Brasil alone, leaving her ensconced in the psychiatric hospital. If she fell apart in Brasil, they would all be in danger. She wasn't stupid.

The beating in her chest started again, but this time it wasn't butterflies, it was a great, big, whopping eagle spreading his wings and flapping in an attempt to fly to freedom. *In through the nose… of course, she remembered… out through the mouth.* She'd barely recovered from a gunshot wound and had deserted her babies, leaving them to the mercy of the man who'd attempted to kill her. The air filled her lungs, she could feel her rib cage expanding to accommodate the air driving a straight line through her diaphragm. The tension in her ribs decreased as she pushed the air back up.

"Of course, I remember. It isn't likely that I would forget." In her head she snarled, a ferocious lion, but she purred the actual words, like a house cat, to keep up the persona of sanity.

"I'm sorry, my darling. I had to ask." The look he gave her filtered through to the functioning part of her brain before the demon stalking her laid claim to her thought process again.

Chapter Twelve

Jose

When next I awoke, my surroundings were familiar. *Mamãe* sat by my bedside flicking through a magazine. I shifted to get comfortable, and her eyes lifted over the top of her magazine which she placed on the table by my bed. "Hey."

"Hey."

"How do you feel?"

"Like I've slept well." I didn't say I felt weaker, drained of all energy despite the sleep.

She bent over and ruffled my hair before placing a kiss on my head.

"Where are the others?"

"Father has taken them back to the hotel."

"Pedro?"

She nodded. "Carlos, too. We talked things out, and will be adopting them both. I hope you're okay with that?"

I smiled.

"So, we just need you to get better and we will have the perfect family." What she didn't say was that it should have been like that from the start.

The doctor came in, and after greeting *Mamãe* and me, he picked up my chart and engrossed himself in the nurses' notes monitoring my blood pressure and temperature. After a few minutes he looked up at me and said, "Jose, we will need to start the dialysis today."

"When can I go home?"

"Let's take each day at a time. You haven't been at all well. The chest infection you developed has made you weak. The antibiotics have started to work, but we need to monitor you. Being out on the streets didn't help your health. You should consider yourself to be one lucky boy that they found you when they did."

It was a few hours later, after drifting in and out of sleep, that a huge contraption was wheeled in. It looked like a basic Tardis machine from *Dr. Who,* with wires and a huge bottle. Apprehension must have shown on my face, because the nurse who accompanied the machine sought to reassure me. *Mamãe* took my hand in hers, and their coldness was a shock to my system.

"You're cold, *Mamãe.*"

"I'm fine, *meu bebê,* never you mind about me. Let's concentrate on making you better."

"You still have to look after yourself, *Senhora.* You should listen to your *filho.* Maybe you can go home and get some rest."

She smiled, a weak tilt of her lips lighting up her beautiful face. "Maybe after the dialysis."

The doctor shook his head as though to argue, but the determined jut of her chin brooked no argument.

"Will it hurt?" My voice trembled as the words spilled out.

"How are you with needles, Jose?"

"Good."

"That is all you will feel."

I rubbed my leg as a sudden cramping pain overtook it, then laughed. "Quit worrying, just a cramp. I get them all the time." A look passed between *Mamãe* and the doctor. "What?"

"Nothing for you to worry about."

"Why the look then?" *Mamãe* informed me this was another symptom of kidney failure. "Just as well I'm about to start dialysis then." I tried to sound casual so as not to worry her with my fears.

Before they started the treatment, a nurse asked *Mamãe* and me to go with her, so that she could weigh me and do a last run through of other checks, all of which were noted in my chart. Any other time, I would've been curious about the chart, as it was about me, but all I could think about was what was going to happen. I didn't know how it would make me feel. *Will it work?* There were questions tumbling around in my brain which hurt my head with the attempt to keep up.

A line was put into my arm while I looked away. It didn't bother me, but I didn't want to watch the needle going in. I barely noticed it, and when I looked back, there were two needles sticking out of my arm. The nurse explained one was to draw my blood away from me, and the other was to bring it back after it had mixed with the dialysate solution, which would pull the toxins out. It was a fascinating process and my enquiring mind wanted to know everything—maybe I'd ask more questions when I felt a bit better.

Pedro

Exhausted, Carlos and I headed to bed. I watched the delight spread over his face when he took in the luxurious bed.

"This and food are what I missed most," Carlos confided while we lay there, and then rushed in with, "I mean apart from my parents."

"S'okay, Carlos, I know that." After a few minutes with only the sound of our breathing breaking the silence, I asked, "Do you mind if I put the reading light on?" When there was no response, I flipped it on. Carlos was asleep in a deep slumber, no doubt the first in many years. I opened up DC's journal, taking out the bookmark I'd found in Jose's drawer, and began reading.

When Leandro, Teo, and I got jobs at the Federal Universidade it was the culmination of one of our dreams. I can't say all our dreams, as we had a lifetime of dreams to achieve, but this was the place where we would be able to work towards them. Teo spent all his time in the lab researching new technologies and studying. It was the adult equivalent of a playground for us. Leandro and I split our time on the campus between the lab and teaching. It was funny hearing ourselves addressed as Professors. It seemed so grown up, yet we didn't feel like adults. I used to joke that we were more like brain chefs, because we fed the minds of eager students. I loved to see their enquiring minds working through and around complex theories and processes. They weren't like children at secondary schools. These young people had chosen the path to further development, so they soaked up what we taught them like sponges. Their keen young minds were also analytical, probing. They would question and challenge us. Some professors of our acquaintance hated that, they felt the students were challenging their knowledge, but Leandro and I loved to debate with these students. Sometimes their passion would fuel an idea that we'd explore further in the lab. Being open to suggestions from them was every bit as important as imparting our knowledge to them. We didn't want to breed a generation who only did as they were told. The future of our civilisation lay in working brains, not ones trained merely to obey.

Many years passed. We worked hard, every day a pleasure containing something new within the same routine. Not only did we work together, but we drank together, and shared meals and laughter. Leandro and Carolina married, as did some of the others. We were content. There were rumblings of discontent all around us, corruption was rife, but we lived in a cocoon which nothing penetrated—or so we thought.

At the lab we began piecing together some data which would be ground breaking—if we got it right. We spoke only to each other about our findings; excitement was an understatement. With each week that passed something else would slot into place, more evidence that we were on the right track.

Carolina announced that she was pregnant. It was a bittersweet moment. My all-encompassing love for her hadn't dimmed through the years. I knew she would never be mine. Had there been the slightest possibility that she might have looked upon me favourably, I wouldn't have entertained it. My love for Leandro was that of a best friend, a soulmate, a brother—albeit without the blood tie—and as such, was more powerful. So, while I knew I could never make her mine, this was yet another affirmation of how impossible my love for her was. At the same time, I was thrilled for her and Leandro. Their love for each other grew stronger every day. I don't think I ever met two people who were so in love. Romeo and Juliet, Mark Antony and Cleopatra, Lancelot and Guinevere, any of the classical lovers, they had nothing on the love Leandro and Carolina shared.

I still remember the rapt expression that lit up her eyes, the tilt of her lips when she imparted her news. It was almost childlike in its innocence, but at the same time a thousand secrets sat in those eyes and the curve of those lips. She hadn't known at the time that she carried twins...

I stopped reading, the implication slamming into me like a gale force wind. Carolina was my *mamãe* and Leandro my *pai*. All along DC had known who I was, but hadn't told me. Turning out the bedside lamp, I began trying to make sense of what I'd read. A multitude of emotions crashed through my consciousness, until my head hurt with the effort of trying to process it.

Why didn't he tell me?

All the comments made in the journal were not describing two random people; they were my parents. They had to be. What had happened to them? I knew I could continue reading and draw the answers from the elaborate script, but at the same time I dreaded discovering something within those pages that I wouldn't be able to handle. I wanted to share this with

Jose. To discover the truth together, but I couldn't place such a burden on his shoulders when he was critically ill.

I lay sleepless for most of the night, trying not to toss and turn as I didn't want to disturb Carlos. At some point I must have slept, though. The next morning I was awoken by Carlos shifting around in bed.

The awe on Carlos' face, when we sat down for breakfast, showed me what mine must have looked like when I'd first encountered the abundance of available food.

"Boys, I am going to spend the day talking to solicitors to arrange your adoption, but I need as much information as possible from you both. Birth certificates, full names, and your date of birth, Carlos."

"We have no paper certificates, and I know nothing. Pedro is the name DC gave me. I don't even know which orphanage I was in, or my birth date—but you would know that from when you took Jose."

"Yes, of course. Pedro, you were born on the twelfth of September, 1981."

I smiled. Learning that tiny piece of information about myself was surprisingly satisfying.

"Carlos, do you know anything that will help us?"

"My full name is Carlos Suarez. My parents were Carlo and Daniela. I don't remember my birthdate—it didn't seem important on the streets—but my house was just off the R. São João Batista, about five minutes from the cemetery."

"That's great, boys. I'm going to drop you off at the hospital, with Jose and Christina. You'll also be accompanied, at all times, by an armed guard. After what you told me about Martinez, I won't risk your safety."

I nodded knowing that it wouldn't make a difference. A private guard had no jurisdiction over a *policial*.

"Pedro, this man is being paid a lot of money to do as I ask him. He will shoot first and ask questions after, including Martinez himself. You needn't worry."

My mouth resembled the letter O when it dropped open.

"You have a very expressive face. You will never make a poker player."

"Poker?"

"I'll explain some other time."

Jose looked exhausted when we arrived. There was a huge machine taking up the space where one of the chairs had been. Two tubes of blood were attached, via needles, to his arm.

I shivered at the sight of the needle. I'd never had one placed in my arm, but where I lived drugs were rife, and bodies of drug addicts often littered the pavement. Drugs were a more lucrative side-line for Martinez than the pickpocketing. He must have made a fortune from all his shady operations. Pimping the boys was another big earner for him. Shivering at the thought, I avoided looking at Carlos for fear he would know what I was thinking. I lay down beside Jose on the bed.

"Come and sit on the end of the bed, Carlos, my new brother," Jose said.

Peals of laughter came from all three of us as we tried to find room for everyone to stay on the bed.

"Be careful, boys," Christina admonished, but her gentle smile softened the rebuke.

Despite the fact that Jose was ill and having blood pumped in and out of his body, we'd never been so carefree. I had no doubts he would get better, now that he was getting the treatment. As much as Fernando thought I couldn't hide my feelings, I hid the turmoil DC's journal had stirred up so that I didn't mar this moment.

"I'm so excited that I have two brothers now," Jose said. "We'll have so much fun."

"I hope you don't all end up too much for us." As soon as the words were out of her mouth Christina blanched and quickly added, "It doesn't matter if you are. You are staying with us."

The Exiles — England

Leandro

Leandro lit a cigarette, then flicked the match with his hand to extinguish the flame before dropping the burnt stick into the ashtray. Stefano, who had returned from his brief trip to Brasil was the centre of attention. The men gathered around the table with their steaming mugs of coffee forgotten, firing questions at Stefano. Their need for information about their homeland was as desperate as an addict for his fix. Leandro stayed silent while the others questioned Stefano, soaking up any information he could glean.

"In many ways nothing much has changed, but then some things are completely alien."

"Like what?"

"Tell us more?"

Leandro's thoughts wandered as he visualised the questions dancing in the air like the stars above a cartoon character's head who's been thumped with a blunt instrument. This made him think of Carolina, who enjoyed watching cartoons like *Tom and Jerry* despite Leandro's opinion they propagated violence. He had endured more than his fair share all those years ago.

"The boys would love it, when they get older of course," *Carolina would say.*

They hadn't had the chance to name their children, and Carolina always spoke of them as though they were still newborn babies. He had wondered more than once whether she thought time was standing still for the twins, even though it hadn't. As though she would be able to scoop tiny babies from the cots where they had left them, not the grown boys they would be now, and assign them names as she held them in her arms.

The men listened agog to Stefano's stories; each one of them wore a tear in his duct that he would not shed.

"So, it is agreed we will go back?" Leandro interrupted their meandering down memory lane.

"Yes. We will leave the women and children here," Teo replied.

"Caro is coming with us."

A gasp spread around the little group.

"Do you think that's wise?" Teo, as spokesperson, voiced their concerns.

"No, but she insists. I can hardly leave her alone here."

"Can't you have her sectioned again?" one of the men asked. What he left unsaid was that none of their wives would entertain the idea of looking after her.

"It isn't a B&B," Leandro snapped, his anger aimed at himself for thinking the same thing.

A silence hung over the group. As he had caused the awkwardness, Leandro asked Stefano a question to allow the conversation to restart. He could almost hear the collective sigh of relief.

"The streets are littered with homeless children, Leandro. Children as young as… well, babies, being touted as begging tools for the tourists. A whole generation of children have grown up on the streets. It is rumoured that the *polícia* go on shooting sprees now to keep the numbers down."

No one spoke now knowing that Leandro's twin boys were as good as orphaned and may well have ended up on the streets. The silence, which should've been comfortable for men who had known each other a lifetime, was stifling. One by one, they made their excuses, until only Teo and Leandro were left. Teo placed a gnarled hand on top of Leandro's to still the quiver.

Chapter Thirteen

Jose

Pedro and Carlos arrived with a burly man who was at least six foot, five inches tall. He made me think of the man whose stabbing I had witnessed. I hadn't told anyone about that—well, other than Carlos.

Chad was an American, a gun for hire. Pedro called him our bodyguard. I shuddered. Chad was, despite his size and job, an affable man. He stood in the corner of my room and surveyed our domestic scene with a benevolent smile. Chad didn't speak much, but when he did it was with a heavy southern drawl. My knowledge of America was limited to the hours of American programmes I'd watched. He wore a security guard uniform, battleship grey trousers, and a jacket. A strap slashed diagonally across the whiteness of his starched shirt announced the holster and the presence of a gun.

A few months ago I would have thrilled at this story, a real life TV programme, it would've seemed, but then I couldn't have foreseen it becoming part of my life. I was scared. I wasn't scared of Chad, whose dark beard covered the lower half of his face, or of the gun he wore, but what it all represented. I knew I was safer right now than I had been on the streets, but I wanted all this to be over. The idea of *Mamãe* being caught up in any of it didn't sit well with me either.

The fear of Martinez, of the possibility that I could die, shouldn't have been a consideration for any twelve-year-old. I pushed this thought aside. I couldn't believe that it had all worked out so well. I wouldn't have to save my pocket money in order to rescue Pedro and Carlos. The truth was, I would never have been able to achieve it, not until I was an adult, and who knew what could have happened by then.

Pedro joined me on the bed, on my left side. My right arm was still attached to the dialysis machine. After only a couple of hours, the clicking and gurgling sound which came from the machine was starting to annoy me. Maybe the boys would provide a welcome distraction. I didn't want them to know how exhausted I was, so I decided to wear a mask for their sake, *Mamãe's* too. The connection between Pedro and me was so acute that I wondered whether he would guess. My lips formed a smile for him. Carlos stood at the foot of the bed, the chair he had sat on yesterday having been replaced by the hunk of noisy metal.

"Come and sit on the end of the bed, Carlos, my new brother."

Mamãe pretended to tell us off when we jostled on the bed to make room for Carlos. We ended up laughing so much that although I refused to admit it, I was feeling light-headed and weak. I tried to hide the shortness of breath by staying quiet for a while. I didn't want her or the doctor to decide these visits were too tiring for me.

The doctor persuaded *Mamãe* to go and get something to eat. "There's a lovely little cafe across the road where you can get *Moqueca* or *Feijoada*. And their *brigadeiros* are *requintado*. I bet if you ask them, they would wrap some more up for the boys. Though Jose can only have a half."

"*Mmm*, chocolate truffles. *Mamãe* you must. Tell her, Pedro. Carlos." I looked from one to the other, and they were both frowning.

It was *Mamãe* who figured out first that they'd never had them before.

"Boys, you are going to love them." She gathered up her bag with an admonition to behave while she was gone.

"Oh, but *Senhora*, I have my orders to look after you."

"Your brief is to protect my sons." Her smiled, reduced the severity of her tone.

Why Father considered her weak was beyond me. Her strength was fearsome. Although, I had to concede that her health wasn't always robust. I could see that Carlos wanted to say something, but his eyes flitted to Chad in the corner.

"He ain't listening," I assured him, sure that Chad had no interest in the conversation of three children.

"I told Fernando and Pedro about…" he stopped, I think he was willing me to understand without him having to say anything.

I realised then what he was saying. "And *Mamãe*?"

"Fernando said he will tell her."

"You're quiet, Pedro? What's up?"

"Why should anything be up? You two are nattering like a couple of girls."

"Pedro, you can't fool me."

Pedro gave an exaggerated sigh. "It's nothing."

"What is?"

"Do you want me to go so you can talk?" Carlos asked.

"Nothing to talk about. Why would we want you to leave?"

"It's just I'm not your proper brother. You two have a bond."

"Look, Jose and I may be twins, and he may be able to tell when I have a problem, and I him, but that doesn't mean you're not our proper brother. You're just the older brother who doesn't share the ESP."

"What's E—" Carlos started, but I cut over him with, "So you *do* have a problem?"

"I don't want to trouble you when you're ill, Jose."

"I'll worry more if you don't tell me. You've seen the kind of imagination I have."

The doctor chose that moment to walk in. "I hope you two aren't tiring him out?" he directed at my brothers.

"No *Médico*," they chorused, reminding me of school assemblies where everyone said *"Morning, Mr. Peters,"* in a chorus which rose and fell in the same places.

"We're going to stop the dialysis machine now, so you two scamps will have to move. Pedro, when your *mamãe* returns, I want you to come with me for the test. We need to see if you are a match, if you are still willing to be a donor, that is?"

Pedro bounced off the bed and nodded. *"Sim, Médico."*

"We will book you in to discuss the procedure first, if you are found to be a match. We need to be very clear so that you understand what you will be doing, the risks you are taking."

"I'll do it anyway, *Médico*. Save the chat and let's do the operation." Pedro wore his stubborn expression.

"We have to go through the whole process, young man." His chocolate-coloured eyes sparkled in Pedro's direction. I guessed he admired Pedro's courage.

Mamãe's shoes tapping a gentle beat on the floor announced her return just as the doctor, assisted by the nurse who'd arrived as well, removed the needles from my arm.

"Two days, we'll do it again, Jose. The nurse will do your observations now."

Pedro

The results of the test would come back the following day, but this was just the first of three. If I were a match, then I would proceed with the other tests. It all sounded complicated. I just wanted to get on with it. It felt like an eternity to me. The sooner I gave my brother my kidney, the sooner he would get better, and then we could move to England—away from Martinez's reach.

I wasn't being brave like everyone thought. I didn't want to think about the process in case it scared me too much. Bravery was the front I wore.

The doctor put a band around my arm and began tightening it until I thought my arm would explode. *Is he trying to burst my blood vessel?* Then I saw the needle. I looked at it. How could something so small create such fear? With some effort, I bit back the cry which longed to escape when the needle pierced my skin. I kept telling myself this wasn't like jacking up on heroin or cocaine. I'd seen too much of that on the streets, the wraiths with the desperation in their eyes. They would do anything for a hit, including selling their souls. Sometimes, I used to think that it would be a blessing for them if that one last hit was fatal. Someone had offered heroin to me once, a free introductory offer. There been a tiny voice in my head which had whispered that I would forget my pain and loss in that rush, but I knew that the path I walked was nothing compared to the hell addicts did, so I told them where to stick their drugs.

Jose looked at me with those penetrating eyes of his when I returned to the room. His enquiry had little to do with the tests, and all to do with quizzing me about what was bothering me. I would not be able to keep it a secret for long.

Later that night, back at the hotel as Carlos drifted back into a deep sleep, I pulled the drawer open and removed the journal.

Eureka! Isn't that how each new discovery is announced. It's a cliché but also apt word. We had stumbled—no, I won't use that word, as it gives the impression that we tripped over it unexpectedly— rather than the hours, the weeks, months, even years that we had devoted to it. We had discovered a source of energy that would power the world over without leaving a scar on the land. It was a harnessing of nature itself, beyond solar power and wind turbines. Every household in the world could benefit, and the cost of harnessing it would be minimal.

What we had was revolutionary, even third world nations would be able to generate this power. With this technology, we could change the world. To say we were excited would be an understatement. To mention we were scared, was also true. Our discovery would make gas, coal, oil, and wood obsolete for this purpose. Trees would not be slaughtered to heat homes. Harmful emissions would not damage the environment. We believed that, with a little bit of tweaking, this technology would also power cars. The drawback? There would be many companies who would no longer function within a decade due to our discovery—and from these people we feared retribution.

We waited with mounting excitement after sharing our find.

"Why the delay?" Leandro would ask.

"This is huge, my friend, give them time to process it," I answered; although I, too, could not understand the silence.

With every day that passed, the tension mounted. Although I reassured Leandro, the lack of communication bothered me.

Carolina was getting closer to her due date but instead of feeling joy, we were apprehensive. We started to argue amongst ourselves. We were seven tense men fraught with tension and feeling as though we were waiting for an axe to fall, when we should have been celebrating. The first rumblings started to filter through that something was amiss. Whispers in the corridors, then Teo's house was turned over. Word finally filtered in from an old school friend of Leandro's. Sebastião, a surgeon of great renown, had family connections in very high places.

We met, in secret, at a house Sebastião owned in Joatinga. Perched on the clifftops, the crash of waves was a constant sound. We travelled separately as instructed. The day was hotter than usual, and we arrived sweaty and irritable. It was all so cloak and dagger. We were scientists, not spies or criminals——excitement for us was in formulae, not in intrigue.

Sebastião greeted us all with wariness. We were there only because of his longstanding friendship with Leandro, and his body language made that clear. "Was anyone followed?"

We all looked at him as though he were crazy.

"What do you know, my friend? Why all this secrecy?"

"My brother-in-law brought me some news. Top secret news. He only told me as he knew you and I are good friends, Leandro. We owe you a life debt for rescuing my sister."

He referred to a time many years ago when they were ten-year olds, Luciana was eight and desperate to gain the attention of her brother and his friend. She had followed them to the forest where they splashed in the **lago**, *racing each other from one side to the other. Both boys were strong swimmers. Luciana snuck up on the friends as they were drying off on the bank. Sebastião told his sister off and commanded her to go home. She turned away, disheartened. Sebastião challenged Leandro to a race and both boys took off. It was a few seconds later that Leandro heard a scream; Sebastião* *continued running having heard nothing. Leandro raced back to the* lago *where he saw Luciana struggling to stay afloat after falling in. Leandro threw himself in, fully clothed, and pulled her to the side. Realising that Leandro was no longer hard on his tail, Sebastião had turned to see where he was. He returned in time to help pull his sister up the bank. Having taken in so much water, Luciana had stopped breathing. Sebastião just stood there frozen in fear while Leandro attempted mouth to mouth. He wasn't sure what he was doing, but a few seconds later Luciana coughed and threw up the water. That had been the deciding factor in Sebastião's career path, and his lifelong promise to Leandro.*

Sebastião cleared his throat and up until that point I have to admit I believed he was enjoying the drama that swirled around his head like a mist, but this belief was dispelled by his next words.

"Your discovery has rattled a great many cages, my friend. Not least of which, the big fuel companies who you will take out of business. All of us here are men of science who thirst after knowledge and advancement.

The vast majority of people in government and in the power houses have no interest in it unless it brings them personal prosperity. The big fuel companies pay kickbacks all the way up the chain, stipends to the policía *and large endowments to the* <u>político</u>. *This goes almost to the top and is the way it has been for many generations. What you have discovered, the proposals you have made, would be a godsend for the populace and the environment. For those in power, what you propose takes away from the fat nest eggs that they are building. They cannot allow it to happen."*

"They cannot stop advancement." You see how innocent I was then? I truly believed it.

"They can arrange accidents for the men who stand in their way."

A collective gasp went around the room in varying pitches.

"You cannot mean that… that they would kill us?" Leandro asked.

"That is exactly what they plan to do. They must silence you. They know threats to be useless. While you

live, you pose a continual threat." He stopped to look around at us all.

No one spoke. A cold shiver swept over me as I tried to process his words which spun around in my head.

"How long do we have?" Leandro asked the question we all wanted the answer to. His face was devoid of any colour, and in the last few minutes he seemed to have aged a decade or more.

A tableau of frozen expressions stared at Sebastião. I thought of a childhood story my mamãe had read to me of a group of children frozen by a wicked snow queen, and in that moment, while I waited for Sebastião's response, I focused on the absurdity of irrelevance.

"A week at the most."

As though the spell was broken, voices tumbled out like clowns tripping all over each other. Outpourings of words, filled with grief and fear stumbling together, and merging into white noise.

"Quiet, men," Sebastião's voice rose above the clamour. "I don't have all the answers, but I do have a contact who, as we speak, is making false identities for you all. We will get you out of the country until it is safe to bring you back. My brother-in-law despises the corruption and is working towards bringing down the key players. He needs to know who he can trust, and must be able to provide irrefutable evidence to do so. When he has done so, then you can all return. You must trust no one. Do you hear me? No one. My name must never be mentioned. I will do all I can to help you, but I will not risk the lives of my family… not even for you, my friend."

Leandro clasped his arm, kissing both cheeks. "Thank you, my friend. We all owe you the debt of life."

"Gather what you need but no more. Take nothing that will betray your real identity. I will get word to you when everything is ready. Be vigilant, but not obvious. I don't think you are being watched at the moment, although I cannot be sure. Go about your normal duties, don't raise suspicion."

Two days later we received an urgent message from Sebastião. It was also the day that Carolina went into *labour. Despite my concerns, Leandro insisted on telling his brother Paolo. He convinced them both that they had to leave the baby behind and flee. He said that he would care for the baby as his own——or his wife would——until their return. I had never trusted Paolo, but Leandro was trusting despite all the evidence to the contrary.*

I knew I could not leave my homeland Brasil; Rio itself was in my blood. I would gather what I had and live off the streets, the ultimate invisibility cloak. We said our goodbyes at the hospital with unshed tears in our eyes. I walked away from Leandro, from Carolina and the hospital, without a backward glance. It was the only way I could do it. I slid into the shadows, and so began my process of melting into the weave of the fabric which makes up the streets.

It was only a matter of hours later when I started feeling uneasy. I should clarify, more uneasy. My stomach churned, waves of nausea crashing against the lining of my abdomen. It had nothing to do with the stench of the streets. A siren whispered my name, her voice growing louder until she sounded like a gull screeching a warning.

I rose and started out on cautious feet which gained momentum until they sped across the uneven paving. My breaths came in gasps as I was unused to the physical exertion. I knew that everything was wrong, but prayed that I would not be too late. I watched as Teo approached the entrance to the hospital from the opposite direction. We stopped to look at each other, and wordlessly, we joined forces.

We heard the rapport of the gun, followed a split second later by another. The sound of steps forced us into a doorway. We pressed into the shadows, flattening ourselves against the wall.

I bit back the cry which yearned to escape when I saw Paolo walk away, slipping the gun inside his shirt. His casual step and grim smile made me long to drive my fist into his face. I made to move the instant he had passed our hiding place, but Teo's hand stayed me. While he dared not speak, his eyes implored mine, boring into them. My heart pounded inside my chest.

How was it possible that he hadn't heard it when, to me, it was deafening?

When Teo's hand dropped down, we both crept out. Knowing what you will find and seeing it are two distinct things. The figures lay prone, side by side, with blood oozing from their bullet wounds..."

Tears rocked me and I stopped reading. There was no doubt in my mind I'd just read the details of my parent's death. That night, when exhaustion overcame me, I fell into a fitful sleep. My dreams were haunted by the deaths of DC and Jonny which became entwined with the deaths of my parents.

I screamed into the darkness.

The Exiles – Brasil

Teo

The rush of heat hit them when they stepped out of the airplane. Teo, who headed the little group, paused for a few seconds to inhale the familiar scents flooding back into his consciousness after so many years in the cold, damp starkness of English shores. Aware of the impatient buzz behind him, he placed one foot in front of the other and descended the metal steps. Rumblings of pleasure echoed around him as the others savoured the feel and smell of home.

Stefano had done well on his scouting mission, finding a few locations on the outskirts of the city where they could stay. Leandro and Caro were staying with Sebastião, and the rest of them would be split between safe houses. Taxis lined up to take them all in their different directions.

As the cars moved off, Teo felt the fear he'd managed to hold at bay until now come crashing down on him. His stomach twisted in knots and his bowels twitched; it took all his willpower to hold himself in check. He slid lower in the seat while the taxi travelled through the crowded streets. It wasn't too much of a stretch to think he might be recognised. Money sat like a bounty on their heads, and he knew that the passage of years wouldn't have changed the threat their knowledge posed. Stefano had spoken to Sebastião's brother-in-law, who had said the time was right, and he had gathered enough evidence to take down all the key players.

Chapter Fourteen

Jose

In order to avoid worrying everyone, I tried to hide how exhausted I felt. I slept a lot, but when I was awake, my thoughts wandered to Pedro. His inverted brows, the faraway look in his eyes, and the tautness of his shoulders all told me something was troubling him. It seemed an age before Pedro and Carlos turned up with their faithful shadow, who smiled at me and acknowledged *Mamãe* with a respectful, "Ma'am." I couldn't ask Pedro what was wrong in front of *Mamãe*, though.

"Are you going to get some food at that cafe today, *Mamãe*?"

"You mean chocolate truffles?" She laughed. "Yes, I suppose I could. I have three boys to spoil now."

"Can I go with you?" Carlos asked. He knew what I wanted to ask Pedro, and probably thought there was more chance my brother would open up to me if we were alone.

"The boys are supposed to be with me." Chad looked worried.

Mamãe tried to assure him, with her promise of, "He'll be fine with me."

The indecision was written all over Chad's face when Carlos spoke up, his voice small and unsure. "Excuse me."

We all turned to him, surprised. Except for with Pedro and me, Carlos didn't talk unless spoken to.

"I think I'll be safe. Martinez doesn't notice me. It's Pedro he'll be angry with."

Chad couldn't argue with that, and so, they left.

"Okay, out with it. You look worse today than you did yesterday," I said as soon as *Mamãe* and Carlos were gone.

"Jose, drop it. It can wait for another time."

"I can't sleep well worrying about you, and with my treatment, I need all the sleep I can get." I played my trump card.

"Not sure you will sleep any better if I tell you."

"Now I *am* worried."

"Okay. I've had a package that belonged to DC. I opened it the other day for the first time and found his journal. Jose, he knew our real parents, Leandro and Carolina. They were killed by Leandro's brother, our uncle, just after we were born."

Of all the things I might've expected him to say, that wasn't on my radar at all. *Our parents*, I had never given them too much thought. The day I met Pedro was the first time I had spoken about them to anyone. To me, they had been the lesser concern as I thought about my new brother, and the situation I believed to be happening with the couple who *had* raised me as their own. Unlike Pedro, I had always known parents—even when I had found out that they weren't my biological parents. Never had I felt the loss of being an orphan. I had felt betrayal and anger. Pedro, on the other hand, only knew being an orphan, so I guess he'd thought about them through the years.

"Say something?" he pressed.

"Did he describe them? You know, what they were like?"

While Pedro poured out everything he knew, a spark flickered inside me. *Leandro* and *Carolina*. I tried their names out in my head. *Mamãe* and *Pai*. Rumblings of guilt churned my stomach as even that thought seemed a betrayal. I confided in Pedro. He lay his head against mine and I lay back onto the plump pillow, exhausted.

"Thanks for telling me," I murmured just as *Mamãe* walked back in with Carlos, who had already eaten a chocolate truffle by the look of him.

"Telling you what?" *Mamãe* looked from one of us to the other.

"Has Pedro had a *brigadeiros* already?" Pedro's diversionary tactic worked.

Father popped in later, and after enquiring about my well-being, asked *Mamãe* to go for a walk with him.

"What's that about?" Carlos asked.

239

"Just talking to *Mamãe*."

"*Hmm*, you really are very innocent, little brother."

"Little brother?" I snorted. "I might have been born first."

After what seemed like forever, they came back in. Silence settled over the room. I think we were all scared about what we might hear next. Father broke the silence by indulging in small talk.

He never did that.

"Any news on the adoption?" Pedro asked.

I realised then that both he and Carlos were waiting for the answer they feared the most. That was what they'd seen when Father and *Mamãe* left the room. Pedro was right; I was innocent. *Would I ever truly understand what they had lived through out on the streets?* A picture of the stabbing flashed through my head, but I pushed it aside.

"Are you okay? Shall I call a doctor?" *Mamãe* rushed to my side.

"Oh, no, I'm fine. Tell us what news you have."

She sighed before making eye contact with Father.

"Yesterday, the solicitor tracked down Carlos' birth certificate, and we were able to trace your uncle, who is your legal guardian," Fernando said.

"Hrumph," Carlos interjected.

"They kicked him out onto the streets, Father. You're not going to make him go back there, are you?"

"No, Jose. We are adopting him. We haven't changed our minds about that. Today, the solicitor and I went to see your uncle, and he has signed papers so that we can become your legal guardians until the adoption is formalised—"

"How much?" Carlos asked.

Father hesitated, not expecting that question and clearly not comfortable answering it.

"How much did he sell me for?"

Mamãe went to his side and wrapped him in her arms, kissing his cheek. "None of that matters."

Carlos had confirmation in her words but the stubborn set of Father's jaw indicated no figure would be discussed.

"I have the solicitor drawing up the paperwork now."

241

"And me?" I'd never heard Pedro's voice to be so unsure.

"We are struggling there, Pedro. When we adopted Jose… let's just say there was very little paperwork. No names of your biological parents, and they'd kept no records at all. All records they did have, were sent to a central base."

"So, I don't exist. Is that what you're saying?"

"We have to do some more digging to find out what your parent's names were."

I looked to Pedro and then nudged him. "Tell them," I hissed.

He shook his head.

Pedro

"Tell them," Jose urged.

I shook my head, then mumbled, "There wasn't anything other than their first names anyway."

"Pedro?" Fernando looked at me while Christina smiled gentle encouragement. So, I told them what I had told Jose.

"Is that what your nightmare was about last night?"

Fernando had rushed in after I'd screamed. Although I'd told him it was only a nightmare, he had held me close until I had drifted back to sleep.

"You read about your natural parents' death and thought you'd keep it to yourself? Oh, Pedro, you can come to us for anything. You don't have to do this alone anymore." Christina's warm eyes held me captive.

I wanted so much to believe I could have a happy ending, but something seemed to always go wrong for me so I didn't dare believe too much. Part of me needed to keep the street kid alive in order to survive, should the worst happen.

"There could be more information in there," Jose said. "You haven't finished reading yet."

"Is that true?" Fernando asked.

I nodded.

"If you want, I will read it with you tonight," Fernando offered.

There was an immense relief knowing that I wouldn't have to go back to the journal alone.

Later that night I brought the journal out to the sofa, clutching it to my chest. My fingers gripped it so tight they'd turned white. Fernando patted the seat beside him, and with tender fingers, prised mine away. Carlos stood up and padded away. Perhaps he figured this was a private matter. When I was ready, Fernando opened the pages. The marker fluttered to the floor, where we left it.

Fernando started by rereading the previous sentence, where I'd left off, and his voice shook. His world didn't include killings. After a tiny pause, he continued…

'"A moan escaped Leandro's lips. I rushed to him, finding him still alive but his face contorted in pain. He mouthed Carolina's name. Teo went to her side. 'She's still breathing. Let's take them into the hospital.'

'No, Teo, they are not safe there. We must take them elsewhere.'

'We should not move them far. We could move the bullets further, and kill them.'

'They will die if we take them in there. Paolo will find them.'

'We can't operate on them.'

'No, but Sebastião can. His house is about sixteen kilometres away. Do you have your car?'

Sebastião opened the door, ushering us in with a look of horror.

We had brought danger to his door but he rallied around once more, taking them both into his home where he performed emergency surgery.

'I have done all I can. The bullets were removed but the next forty-eight hours will be critical for them both.'

Teo and I took turns to watch over Leandro and Carolina that night while Sebastião went to bed, exhausted. The next day, Teo went back to the temporary safe house which Sebastião had arranged while waiting for the false papers. I headed back to the streets.

'Come with us, Daniel?' he offered, but I just shook my head and walked away.

It was two weeks later that they were pronounced well enough to move. Every day I trudged the sixteen kilometres there and back. I had considered putting down roots locally, but it was a well-heeled area and vagrants were not acceptable. It would have been the quickest way for me to have ended up in the hands of the polícia.

We said another farewell when I helped them into Teo's car. This time, I stood in the middle of the road while the dust disturbed by the car eddied around my worn out shoes and trousers. They were headed to the airport, the papers were all in order and they would be boarding a plane for England—'''

"They're alive," I breathed out, interrupting Fernando.

"Maybe, Pedro."

"What do you mean maybe? You just read it out to me." My angry words slashed the air. I so wanted them to be alive.

"We don't know what happened to them after that."

"It might say…" I trailed off realising the possibility DC had been keeping contact with them was slim.

"Let's read on," Fernando said.

"You don't want them to be alive," I accused.

"Why would you say that, Pedro?"

"Cos then it will mean Jose and I will go and live with them."

Fernando pulled me into his arms and held me as I cried great gulping sobs. I heard the patter of feet when Carlos came to investigate my distress. Without a word, he turned and left me to my shame. Taking up the journal, Fernando began reading once more.

"I yearned to board the plane with them, to escape to a different country and be a different person, but I'd made my decision and knew I couldn't cope with being away from my homeland.

I went back to the hospital about a week later—time on the streets loses all meaning, but I think the timescale was accurate. A woman I had dallied with worked there as a nurse. I'd once asked her to marry me, but she'd seen the way I looked at Carolina whenever she was around.

"I don't mind you loving another woman, Daniel, but when I marry, I need to be the only one in the man's heart." She had since met a man who adored her with every fibre of his being, but she admitted to me in a moment of candour that she didn't feel the same, her heart belonged to me.

It took two days of waiting in the shadows before I saw her on her way to work. I had started to fear that she might no longer be there. I called out her name and put my fingers to my lips to warn her I needed discretion.

'Daniel, what are you doing here?'

I filled her in with as much as I could, without saying too much.

'Those twins belong to Leandro and Carolina?'

I could barely contain my anger when she told me that one of the boys had been adopted from the orphanage where a friend of hers worked. The other boy had been left there. I asked her to get me any information she could on the couple and to keep me up to date on the baby in the orphanage. I had to try to keep track of them.

'I can't access the orphanage's records, if they even kept any. I certainly can't ask my friend to without raising suspicion. If it's as dangerous as you say…' she answered, and I knew that at least one of the babies was beyond my help.

I told her where she could find me. Once a week I would be there in case she had any news. I reiterated the need for her to say nothing to anyone with a firm, "My life depends on your silence.'

Every week I went to the meeting point but she never came, and I began to think Adriana was too scared to get involved. A year went by. I had begun to scavenge old newspapers. It kept me up to date with what was happening in the world and enabled me to watch the passage of time.

Then, one week she was standing at the corner, looking furtively around her. I remember seeing her eyes darting everywhere, and so mine did the same to make sure that it wasn't a set up.

'Daniel?' she whispered when she saw me. Her hand reached up and touched the growth of hair on my face. Gone was the smooth shaven skin she'd known, it was no longer a priority on the streets. It also added warmth and a layer of incognito.

I cut straight to the chase, no small talk or niceties as I asked about the baby.

The baby hasn't been adopted. He is of no more financial use to the orphanage.'

I sucked in my breath at her words.

'I know, Daniel,' She sighed. 'But that is the world we live in.'

'So, what will they do now?'

'There is an aléia at the back of the North end, Av. Luís Carlos Prestes, a few blocks away from the orphanage. They leave the unwanted babies there.' She went on to give me the time and location, describing what I would see. 'What will you do, Daniel?'

'The only thing I can do. I will look after the baby.'

'You, Daniel?' It had sounded like an accusation. 'How can you look after a baby?'

'I will find a way. I will protect him with my life.'

'It was always her.'

'It isn't only about her, Adriana. Leandro was my best friend.'

'Okay. Come back tomorrow. I will bring supplies.'

I thanked her before heading off into the maze of favelas, now as familiar to me as my own body.

That night I watched the aléia before dusk set upon Rio. I needed to be there early to ensure nothing untoward happened. I slunk into the shadows and waited until the men came to drop off the baby. As the sun went down, the burnt umber of the sky mixed with pinks and purples creating something so beautiful it was hard to believe that something so despicable was happening. They walked away without a backward glance, as though they had merely been throwing out rubbish. The sounds of Rio coming to life drowned out the heavy thumping of my heart. Music throbbed and raucous voices flaunted a side to my city I had never been part of. Scurrying over, I found two babies curled up in blankets on the dingy step. Fear clawed at me that I might pick the wrong one. Even had I been sure, I could not have left one behind.

It did not take me long to know which baby belonged to Leandro and Carolina. I named him Pedro, and the other baby I called Jonny. In some ways it made up to Pedro for losing his twin brother. I met Adriana the next day, and then once a week from then on, which continued for about five years. She gave me a bag of supplies. It wasn't enough to survive on, but it ensured my boys always had something. What I had to learn was how to pick the pockets of the wealthy when the money I had ran out. It was surprising how long a small sum of money lasted on the streets. The only real necessities on the streets were food and warm clothing, for when the nights turned chill.

Pedro and Jonny were my greatest pleasure in life, they were what made me function. I watched them grow like any proud pai. *I educated them. When I got the chance to reunite Pedro with his parents, I wanted them to see how clever he was. Jonny was a bright pupil, too, but Pedro excelled in everything. To him, it was easy; he soaked it up like a sponge. He loved it. His memory was phenomenal, too, whereas Jonny had to work harder to achieve even half of what Pedro accomplished. His intelligence had been inherited from Leandro, and his compassion and love reminded me of Carolina. When the boys played, I would declare Jonny the winner at times so that he, too, could feel the pleasure of accomplishment. Being in Pedro's shadow was not easy. Pedro always knew that he'd beaten Jonny but would congratulate him anyway, and then look to me for approval. He never had to look far.*

The years passed, and I heard nothing from Leandro. I did not even know whether they still lived. I longed to see them again, to show them Pedro, but at the same time I dreaded losing the boy I now thought of as mine."

Fernando stopped and looked at me. "There is no more now."

I stayed silent, tired but also conflicted by the emotions I'd never experienced before.

"He sounded like an amazing man."

The tears fell again, a silent colony of ants marching down my cheeks to splatter Fernando's shirt front.

The Exiles – Brasil

Teo

The men all met up in secret a week after arriving back in Brasil. Each day, Teo ventured out with his heart beating at a furious pace inside his chest, but the pleasure of being back in his homeland outweighed those fears. As the week wore on, he strode with more confidence. The tastes, sounds, and smells warmed his heart. He wished that his wife were here with him; her homesickness was acute, but she never complained. His

253

three children had been born in England. The only thing they knew about Brasil was from the stories he told them.

Everyone sat around in a circle while smiles lit up their faces, although fear stalked their eyes.

"I'd like to introduce my brother-in-law Ramon Barbosa to all those who don't know him," Sebastião said holding his hand out to a short, wiry man sporting a pencil moustache.

"*Bom Dia*, everyone. You have all suffered much by being exiled from our country. I haven't forgotten how much of a sacrifice this has been for you all. Rest assured, I haven't been idle during this time. I now know who I can trust, and who is caught up in this duplicitous circle of corruption. I have approached a few people and, together, we have gathered enough evidence. We are drafting in forces from outside of Rio. When we take them down, it has to be simultaneously, a multi-pronged assault. We don't want any of them to be tipped off and escape."

Everyone talked at once, with a level of excitement that hadn't been present since they'd first made their discovery. Teo looked around. He didn't want to get too excited; believing all was well had been their downfall before.

"We must try to find out what happened to my sons, and Daniel, too."

Teo's jaw tightened at Leandro's words. *It's always about Daniel.*

Chapter Fifteen

Jose

Unable to sleep, I lay there going over in my mind what Pedro had told me about our biological parents. *Shouldn't I be feeling something?* But I didn't. He'd told me they were dead, and although I acknowledged to myself how sad that was, I couldn't *feel* it—no matter how hard I tried. I even tried to make myself cry because that's what people did, but I couldn't do that either. Anger soon replaced the guilt. At Pedro for telling me, at myself for insisting, and at those two people who'd given me life that I knew nothing about and felt nothing for.

I looked across at *Mamãe,* again in the armchair. It couldn't be comfortable for her to lie there night after night, but she refused to leave me. *Why had my so-called real parents left Pedro and me?* If they were any kind of parents, they would not have deserted us. Thinking back to when I was younger, I recalled *Mamãe* had a squishy chair in my room that she used when she'd read to me. When my eyes drooped, she would scoop me up into her arms and lay me on the bed with a kiss on my brow. Whenever I was ill, she would stay in that chair all night, never leaving my side.

Her lashes fanned against her skin as they fluttered open. Our eyes met. I smiled at her as she reached her hand out across the bed and took mine.

"Are you okay, *meu bebê?*"

"Yes, *Mamãe. <u>Eu te amo</u>.*"

A smile lit her face as she reached over and planted a kiss on my forehead. "*Eu te amo* too, *meu bebê.*" She sat back down but kept hold of my hand.

I smiled at the mix of English and Portuguese that we used. We used to joke that it was Enguese or Portuglish. I wondered whether our relationship would change now I had two new brothers. It had to, of course, but that didn't mean I wanted it to. In that moment I wanted her to myself, even if that weren't reasonable. Part of me wondered if we could go back to before we'd come to Brasil, when everything was normal. But it wasn't normal. My illness was something I hadn't known about. Now I did. Nor had I known I had a brother then, but now I felt complete. Of course I wouldn't want to go back to the time before I knew of his existence. It was probably just the treatment making me clingy and possessive.

"Jose?"

"Yes, *Mamãe*?"

"You seem distracted. Are you... are you thinking about your biological parents?" From the way she tripped over her question, I didn't need to look at her to know that she was hurting.

"No, *Mamãe*," the words rushed out of me.

"You know it's okay if you are, right? It would be perfectly understandable. You must have some questions."

"No, *Mamãe*."

"Well, if you do, you can ask."

"I'm tired now." I hated lying to her, but couldn't bear to hurt her by asking anything. Even if I'd had any questions, I was sure she couldn't have answered them.

I tried to stay still; I didn't want her to know I couldn't sleep. A dull band tightened around my head. Although I tried to will them away, the thoughts continued galloping around inside my head with no release, and nowhere to go.

Pedro

"Jose's shoes are too tight for you, Pedro. Why didn't you tell me?"

I'd fallen asleep on the sofa but woken up in the morning on my bed, under the covers, and clothed except for my shoes, which Fernando must have removed.

"I didn't want to complain."

"We'll get your feet measured and have some made to fit you. Like we did for Carlos." He looked as though he were about to say something else then changed his mind.

"Fernando?"

"Yes, Pedro?"

"Do you think..?" I hesitated. "Well, I thought… maybe… can we see if we can find Sebastião?"

"To see if he knows whether your parents are still alive?" I could hear the sad note in his tone.

"Yes, but he would also know my surname, in order for you to adopt me."

"That's a really great idea."

It had pleased him. I knew now why Jose was so eager to make him happy. *What if my parents are still alive, though? Who will my allegiance be to?*

"I will speak to my solicitor, get him to track Sebastião down, and then I will pay him a visit."

"Fernando?" He waited for me to speak. "Can I come with you to visit him?"

Fernando looked as though he were about to refuse me, but I wore a pleading expression. "We had better make sure you have properly fitting shoes for the occasion."

I threw myself at him and hugged him tight before sitting back down, aware that I hadn't requested permission to leave the table.

"We'll drop you off at the hospital, Carlos. I'll see if Chad can recommend another guard."

Finding Sebastião was easy, with him being a renowned surgeon who hadn't moved from the mansion in Joatinga that he'd inherited from his father.

The hire car pulled up at the biggest house I had ever seen. Fernando drove, I sat in the back while Chad sat in the passenger seat. His eyes seemed to scan from left to right then back again, a continuous sweeping movement as his head swung like a pendulum set to slow motion.

A tingle spread up my back when I exited the car, it was as though eyes watched me. I glanced around but didn't see anyone.

261

Fernando placed his hand on the small of my back. "Ready?"

The door was answered by an immaculately dressed woman, her hair was pulled back in a severe bun and her eyebrows arched high. At first I thought her expression was because of our intrusion, but they didn't go back down. Her voice was cultured, a little bit like Christina's, but not as gentle.

"We're here to see *Senhor* Rodrigues," Fernando stated.

"What business do you have with my husband?"

"*Senhora* Rodrigues, the business is quite delicate."

"If you have need of his services, you should attend the hospital…"

"No, *Senhora*, you misunderstand. The delicate nature is not medical, but personal."

She stood there, a dragon guarding a stash of treasure such as DC had described in his stories. I almost expected to see little tendrils of smoke curling from her nostrils.

"What do you want with me that you rudely invade my home?" a deep male voice rumbled from behind her.

262

The man who stepped forward stood well over six feet tall, towering over Fernando, who wasn't exactly short.

"Forgive our intrusion, *Senhor* Rodrigues. What we come to you about is of the utmost importance to us and is extremely delicate."

"You've brought an armed guard with you. Is this how you approach someone in peace?"

"The guard is for protection, not as a threat to you or your family. If you would allow us to come inside, the guard will wait outside?"

The man looked away from Fernando and his eyes lit on me for the first time. His brows knit together. "Come in, then."

We were taken to a room twice the size of the living area in the hotel suite. The chairs were stiff and upright, and looked like they would break if a heavy person sat on them.

"Benedita, dear, can you bring refreshments for… sorry, I don't know your names?"

"An oversight on my part. My name is Fernando Sanchez, and this is Pedro."

She returned with a tray containing tea and cake, and for me a freshly-squeezed, refreshing lemon drink a few minutes later.

"Now, Fernando, please let's cut to the chase."

"I believe you used to know a couple by the names of Leandro and Carolina."

Sebastião's face blanched and his wife's hand trembled, almost causing her to drop the dainty cup. It rattled against the little plate it sat on.

"Who are you? And, please, don't tell me your name again. I want to know who you really are." A steel-edged tone had entered his voice. There was no pretence of friendliness now.

I shivered, fearful of this man.

"It's okay, Pedro," Fernando reassured me before turning to face Sebastião and *Senhora* Rodrigues. "Twelve years ago my wife and I adopted a baby here in Brasil. We named him Jose. The boy had a twin, but fearing for my wife's delicate health, I refused her pleas to allow us to take them both."

He paused to ensure I was okay, and I nodded.

"Our son Jose became ill and needs a kidney transplant. We left England, returning to Brasil to see whether we could track down his twin. I won't go into the details now, but suffice it to say, we found him. Pedro here is his twin. I am ashamed we did not take him as a baby, which as a result of, he ended up living on the streets."

Senhora Rodrigues' hand flew to her mouth and her eyes widened.

"Pedro has forgiven me for this. My wife and I plan to adopt him and bring him into the family he should have been a part of from the start. Pedro was looked after by a man he knew as DC. DC was killed protecting him, but he left a journal behind, which we have read. You knew this man as Daniel Cortez."

The expression on their faces told me that we were on the right track.

"Daniel named Leandro and Carolina as the boys' parents. He mentioned you, too. I believe you saved their lives, which is why we are here now. I don't know if you have any knowledge of whether they are still alive or not, but regardless, we were hoping to find out his surname so we can trace down his paperwork and formally adopt him."

Sebastião and his wife exchanged looks, a silent conversation taking place in the air between them. "We do know the people you speak of," Sebastião said.

"Do know? Not *did*?" I asked, my breath suspended in my chest.

"You are certainly Leandro's son." He chuckled. "Did this journal mention why they fled Brasil?"

"Yes, it did," Fernando answered.

Sebastião sucked in his breath, a short, sharp intake.

"You can trust us."

"Why the bodyguard?"

"A dangerous man poses a threat to Pedro and Carlos."

"Carlos?"

Fernando explained where Carlos came into the story.

"Do you plan on taking all our children from Brasil?"

"Better that than leaving them to starve and be killed by *polícia*."

"*Polícia*? Is it a *policial* who poses a threat to Pedro?"

Fernando nodded.

"His name?" He looked as though he already knew the answer.

"Martinez—"

"Oh, *meu Deus,*" Sebastião and his wife cried out in unison not waiting for any more information.

"You know him?"

Sebastião rose to his feet pressing his shaking hands against the arm of the chair to help him rise. "Please wait."

His wife sat rigid, as though she had turned into a statue.

It seemed an age before Sebastião returned, and he was accompanied by another man.

Fernando grasped my hand, confused as I was by the turn of events. *Is this man a threat? Had DC been wrong about Sebastião?*

The man's face was tired but kindly, lines creasing his eyes as he smiled. I caught my breath at the expression in the honey-tinted eyes which resembled Jose's and mine. The realisation struck me a millisecond before

Sebastião said, "Leandro, this young man is one of your sons. Daniel gave him the name Pedro."

"After my *pai*," he whispered and took a step closer to me.

I could feel my heart pounding in my chest while I rose on unsteady feet. Fernando's hand cupped my elbow, giving me more than physical support. After all these years, I stood before my *pai*. My own body was unrecognisable as every part of it reacted to this man. Tears rose to shame me.

Leandro placed firm hands on my shoulders. He seemed to be drinking in the sight of me. When he had seen everything he needed to, he swept me into a bear hug, his grip tight. "*Meu filho, meu filho,*" he repeated the words over and again as though he had to convince himself.

Between Fernando, Sebastião, and me, we filled *Pai* in on the story. He sat on one side of me, clasping my hands between both of his, while Fernando sat on the other. I could feel the tension coming from Fernando.

"Please tell me, does Daniel live?" Hope filled Leandro's eyes.

268

Huge sobs rocked his feeble frame when I told him what had happened to Daniel. I tried to comfort him as best as I could. I looked to Fernando feeling a little uneasy.

"Who did it?"

"It was organised by a *policial*, by the name of Detective Inspector Martinez."

Leandro responded in the same way that Sebastião and his wife had.

"You know this man." It was more of a statement from Fernando this time.

"*Sim, sim*. In Daniel's journal, did he write what happened to Carolina and me?"

I nodded. "You were both shot by your brother," I stumbled over the words, uncomfortable.

"Yes, Pedro, that is correct. Let me introduce myself to you properly. My name is Leandro Martinez."

I gasped, and my head swam as waves of dizziness swirled around my brain.

"Pedro." Fernando's voice was filled with concern. His face came in and out of focus. "Take deep breaths, *meu filho*." He crushed me against his chest, stroking my hair, speaking soothing words until my breathing regulated again.

"May I ask why you hired a bodyguard when my brother does not know who you are?"

"Martinez runs the crime in the area. Pedro was one of his best pick-pockets. Without going into all the details now, he found out that Pedro had a twin. The look he gave, and the stories Pedro told, made me realise that he was a dangerous man. I could see he didn't want me to take Pedro."

They talked for hours discussing how to handle the situation, although no one mentioned who we would now live with. I think the idea of discussing it scared everyone.

"And Jose? You say he is ill?"

"He needs a kidney transplant." Fernando's response was guarded.

"I'm giving him one of mine if I'm a match," I said, hoping that *Pai* would be proud.

"No, it should be me," *Pai* insisted.

"*Paí?*" I tried the words out on my tongue, happy with the way it rolled off. "Can I ask… what happened to *Mamãe*? Did she… " I couldn't finish.

"She's here, *Filho*." He stopped and looked at Sebastião before continuing, "Your *Mamãe* is not well. Losing you and your brother, being shot, her mind—well, it isn't what it should be."

"Can I meet her?"

"Yes, but I don't want you to get upset if she says or does anything funny. I'll take you to her in her room. With everyone in here, she will be overwhelmed."

"I'm coming, too," Fernando asserted.

The room we entered was similar to the one we'd been in, but it looked more comfortable. The chairs were softer, and some were even big enough to sit three people. A woman sat reading a book. She had once been beautiful, and remnants of that beauty still remained.

She lifted dull, tired eyes up when she heard us. "Leandro," her voice lilted with a soft cadence. "When are we going to the hospital to pick up my babies?"

271

"Caro, darling, remember they were babies twelve years ago."

"I know when they were born, Leandro." She paused and looked straight at me. "Who are you and why are you staring at me?"

"Caro, this young man is one of our sons. His name is Pedro."

"He can't be, Leandro. Our sons were babies. We didn't get to give them names. They are still where we left them. At the hospital."

I took a step toward her, and she stared at me, fear flooding her dilated eyes.

"Don't be scared, *Mamãe*." Keeping my voice low, it was soothing like I used to do for Jonny. I knelt down and took her hands in mine.

She sat docile except for a quiver on her lips. Scars marked the tops of her hands and up her arm, until the sleeve of her dress obliterated my view.

"Look at me, *Mamãe*. I have grown a lot since you last saw me. It must be hard to imagine I was the baby you once held for such a short time. If you look at me, you will see I have *Pai's* eyes, and your mouth and nose."

Her hand, as delicate as a butterfly, fluttered onto my nose and mouth. "But I didn't give you a name."

"Daniel looked after me. He named me after my *avô*."

"Where's your brother?" Her words were expressed in a childlike fashion.

"He isn't well. He's in the hospital."

"What's wrong with him? Was he shot?"

"He needs a kidney transplant, my love," *Pai* answered.

She nodded. "We'll give him one. We can do that, can't we, Leandro?" Her brows knitted together.

"Yes, my dear, I think we can."

"Who are you?" She turned on Fernando.

"I've been looking after Jose… and Pedro."

"Who's Jose? Where's Daniel?"

"Jose is our other son. He went to live with Fernando and his wife while Pedro went to Daniel," *Pai* explained.

"Where is Daniel?" she asked again, her voice rising in agitation.

"Daniel died."

"Hah! I told you he was dead. You didn't believe me because you think I'm crazy. He thinks I'm crazy."

She'd confided the last to me.

The Exiles – Brasil

Leandro

Arriving back in Brasil twanged the strings of his heart
and soul. He breathed in deeply of the sights and sounds.
Everything was so different in England. Years of pining
for his homeland culminated in the moment when his
feet touched home soil. The taxi took him and Carolina
to a point that had been prearranged. After the car pulled
away, another pulled up. Sebastião stepped from the car,
he didn't seem to have aged at all—especially in
comparison to his peer Leandro, whose suffering had
etched its toll on him. The two men hugged, thumping
each other on the back. Tears streamed down their eyes.

"My friend, I owe you my life." Leandro pulled back
and clasped his friend's shoulders, leaning in to kiss both
cheeks.

"I am happy to see you looking so well… and you, Carolina."

She stared at him with a blank expression. "Are you taking me to see my babies?"

Leandro watched Sebastião's brow arch. Aside from one brief postcard sent when they had landed in England, they hadn't communicated since. Leandro had feared implicating Sebastião. The postcard had been cryptic, with no signature.

The two men sat up talking long into the night after they settled Carolina into her room, where, exhausted, she'd gone straight to sleep. Sebastião brought a crystal decanter into the formal lounge with a couple of matching tumblers. He poured the amber liquid into each glass, quarter filling. He held one out to Leandro and took the other. "*Saúde.*"

"*Saúde.*"

The glasses clinked together.

"Tell me about Carolina?" Sebastião asked.

Every night, once the women had retired, the two friends discussed everything from their lives to politics, and everything else in between. Sebastião told Leandro about his brother-in-law's work, which would be culminating in major arrests soon.

Leandro's pleasure was dulled by the lack of leads to any information about his boys. Although he had to be subtle, they had put feelers out and no information was forthcoming. Leandro's fears for Carolina rose to the surface as he watched her enthusiasm wane when the demons planted seeds of unrest in her head.

Despite the inner peace Leandro experienced being back home, and the contentment in talking to Sebastião, there remained a deeper scar which represented what he didn't know. It was all he could do not to scour the streets looking for his boys, but he knew that would get him nowhere. Sebastião's brother-in-law had assured Leandro that as soon as the arrests had been made, he would put all his resources into finding the boys. Until then, any questions in the wrong quarters would place everyone's life is danger. Leandro worried, too, for Carolina's delicate health. In his heart he had known that she could not withstand the pressure of this trip.

The sound of a car engine interrupted his thoughts.

"Stay out of the way, my friend, until I can get rid of them. Make sure Carolina doesn't wander from her room," Sebastião warned.

It seemed like an eternity before Sebastião came back for Leandro and asked him to follow him.

"The people are still here?"

"Yes, my friend, but I think you will want to meet them."

Leandro knew the boy in his heart straight away. Looking at him was like looking at an amalgamation of Carolina and himself. However, it took a few moments for that knowledge to filter through. He had to fight the urge to grab the child and hold him close so that he didn't frighten him. Leandro had warned Caro again and again about not expecting to see a baby, and yet his brain was struggling to assimilate the sight before him. A man, the boy's guardian, stayed by his side like an ever-watchful sentinel. Leandro watched the ease of their interactions with all the comfort of a blade piercing his heart. His son was a boy grown, an intelligent young man, and he had missed out on all of it. Paolo hadn't just tried to take his and Carolina's life, he had denied them both the chance to get to know their sons, to watch them grow and mould them.

The hardest thing for Leandro was listening to his son tell him about the hell he'd lived through on the streets and how ill his twin was. Leandro showed suitable remorse when he learned of Daniel's death, allowing tears to flow, but he did not want to grieve for his lifelong friend and brother of his heart in front of anyone else. He would allow the pain out later, when he was alone.

Leandro watched as Pedro interacted with Carolina, displaying patience and love beyond his years. An overwhelming surge of love rose up inside him. The childlike innocence of his wife was a stark contrast to the street-wise experience of their child. Pedro knelt in front of her, holding onto her hand, and then, with slow and infinite care, he drew her out and gained her reluctant trust.

An insidious whisper curled inside Leandro's brain but he pushed it aside. He couldn't have a favourite.

Chapter Sixteen

Jose

The day dragged without Pedro to keep us amused. Carlos hadn't said much beyond, "He's gone out with your *pai*."

It was early evening when Father and Pedro arrived. I noticed the difference in Pedro straight away as he seemed more animated than I'd ever seen him. It was as though he hugged a delicious secret to himself.

"Where have you been?"

They exchanged glances like conspirators, and I felt a tiny stab of jealousy. They already seemed to have a strong bond which I felt excluded from.

"We've spent the day with our real… erm… biological parents," Pedro stumbled over the distinction.

"I thought you said they were dead?"

"Didn't Carlos fill you in?"

Everyone looked at Carlos, who shrugged, conscious of all the attention on him. "I didn't think it was my place to say anything. And I didn't know they were definitely alive or that you'd met them."

"You're part of this family now," I said. "We're all one big happy family."

"What happens now that *Mamãe* and *Pai* are here?" Pedro asked.

"We already have a *mamãe* and father, and we'll stay together as one big family." I felt my irritation rising.

"But they want us back," Pedro said in earnest.

"Did they say that?" I asked

"No, but I know they do."

"Pedro's right, they do," Father added.

"Fernando, how can you say that?" *Mamãe* sounded scandalised.

"I'm not saying anything other than Pedro is right, they want the boys back. I'm not saying I will allow it."

280

"They're our parents," Pedro asserted angrily.

"They didn't bring us up," I argued.

"They didn't have a choice. Fernando and Christina didn't bring me up," Pedro shot back.

What he didn't add was that they *did* have a choice.

"Boys, this is a unique situation and somehow the adults will work out what the best solution is… ut… ut. No, I don't want to hear any more. When the time comes, we will listen to your opinions too," *Mamãe* asserted without allowing either Pedro or me to argue further.

I simmered.

"Fernando, Christina I'm sorry. I didn't mean to sound ungrateful. I'm just so confused." Pedro gave them a sad smile.

"I know, which is why we will take time over this and work it out together," Father reassured.

I felt my anger subside then at Pedro's words and patted the bed for him to join me. He bounded up like a puppy.

"What are they like?" I asked unable to contain the curious streak which ran through me.

"I have *Pai's* eyes and *Mamãe's* nose and mouth. As yours are the same as mine, then you do too, but I think the shape of your eyes are a bit more like *Mamãe's*. I think you also have her smile, that dimple you get."

He went on to explain more about their lives and the problem Carolina had with her mental health. When he told me what she had said, I was in awe of his response. I'm sure I wouldn't have known what to say. His voice was so full of enthusiasm that my heart felt torn in two.

"They want to come see you."

"They are also insistent that they get checked to see whether they would be a compatible donor, instead of Pedro," Father added.

It felt strange knowing there was a couple out there who loved me but whom I'd never met. Well, except when I was born, and I was hardly going to have any recollection of that. Though cautious, my overriding emotion was fear. I'd had twelve years with *Mamãe* and Father, and I didn't want to be given over to these strangers. *Mamãe* had stayed quiet the whole time. The darkening of her eyes showed she was as scared as me.

While I tossed and turned in my bed that night, I also heard *Mamãe* moving continuously on her chair.

"I'm scared, *Mamãe*," I whispered.

"What of, *meu filho*?"

"What if they insist we go and live with them?"

"Father won't allow it. I won't allow it. You are our *filho* and nothing will change that."

"And Pedro?"

She sighed. "He is different. We will do all we can to keep you together, but we didn't adopt him. He hasn't lived his whole life with us. Hopefully, if they are good people, they will see what is best for both of you and not think of their own needs."

"*Mamãe*?"

"Yes, Jose."

"Would you come up here and hold me till I sleep? Like you used to, please?"

I fell asleep resting against her chest and feeling more confident that everything would work out for the best.

It felt as though a whole flock of birds were beating inside my chest.

A couple walked in with Pedro, and the flapping subsided to a gentle flutter as they both approached me with expressions of love, nerves, and excitement written over their faces as clearly as words encased in the pages of a book. Something familiar pulled at my heart, so tiny that I just barely noticed it. It wasn't as strong as the pull I'd felt when I met Pedro, but it was there nonetheless.

"Jose, I am your *pai* and this is your *mamãe*."

I shook my head.

"*Pai,* remember Jose has known Fernando and Christina as his parents for the last twelve years. He isn't ready to call you that."

Carolina's face dropped and a tear formed in the corner of her eye, which I hated seeing.

Mamãe, who'd been sitting back watching this exchange, introduced herself. "Maybe, Jose, you could call Leandro and Carolina, Mum and Dad, as they do in England?"

A tremulous smile wobbled on Carolina's lips. I had no reason to hurt the people who had given me life. They hadn't had any choice about leaving us, but why had it taken them twelve years to come looking for us?

"Mum and Dad," I tried the words out loud. *Mamãe* knew they had no meaning to me, as I had never called her or Father that, so it was merely a way to make this couple happy.

"*Meu filho*," Carolina whispered. "You are very much like your pa–dad. You and Pedro are almost identical but for the eyes."

"Jose, it is a dream come true to see you again. You have no idea how much Caro and I have longed to be reunited with you and Pedro. To think you were in England, as we were, all that time."

I could see they were both getting emotional. Pedro, too. Apart from the tiny stirring, I felt quite detached. Whether this was natural or whether I was cold, I don't know. Pedro came to my side and lay next to me as he did so often now. I pressed my head to his.

Carolina burst into tears. Leandro rushed to her side and held her close. With gentleness, he stroked her long black hair and whispered to her.

"I'm sorry," she said. "When they placed you in your cot at the hospital your heads were touching, as they are now. The memory made me very sad. Not a day has gone by that I have not longed to hold you again. Every second of every day I've felt your loss in my heart. From the moment I walked away from you, until now, I have not known a moment of joy."

Mamãe got up and crept from the room. I knew she wanted me to be able to bond with them without feeling guilty as she looked on.

"Do you have any other children? Do we have any other brothers or sisters?"

A dark cloud scudded across her eyes and I thought that she was going to cry again.

"After your m–mum was shot, she was unable to conceive again."

The ice which had formed around my heart in an attempt to stop me from feeling anything started to melt watching their evident distress. They had lost Pedro and me, been shot, fled their homeland to set up in a foreign land, and then, to top all that off, had been unable to bear more children. Suddenly twelve years didn't seem so long. How could a person live through that and still come out sane? Although, from what Pedro had said, Carolina's mind had been affected.

An urge to hug them both swept over me but as soon as I felt it, I pushed it aside. *Mamãe* had left so I could bond with them, but in my head that was a betrayal, so I held back and hoped the feeling would pass.

Mamãe came back a short while later accompanied by the doctor.

"Hello, young man. We have the results of the compatibility test we did on your brother. We have found some anomalies, so we would like to do an x-ray to find out some more information. However, I suspect we won't be able to use Pedro."

"You must test us," Leandro insisted.

"Are you related? The best chances are with near relatives."

"We are his biological parents, Doctor. We ask that you keep this information to yourself. If you can just refer to us as near relatives, all our lives will be safer."

The doctor's face turned pale. "If you are criminals—"

"No, Doctor, we are not. We are honest, law-abiding citizens, but unfortunately our wonderful country is not run by people who have the same morals."

287

The doctor took a second to process Leandro's words. "I won't disagree with you, my friend, but for the sake of my own health, I won't speak out about those in power. You understand?"

"We're not here to challenge authority. We just want to save our *filho's* life. *Sim?*"

"I'll arrange for you both to be tested."

Pedro

In my head, I visualised an emotional reunion where *Mamãe*, *Pai*, Jose, and I ended up hugging, kissing, and crying tears of joy—*and I thought Jose was the innocent one*. I had loved DC and Jonny, who were the only family I'd known, even if they weren't blood family. My nights had been spent dreaming of a reunion such as this. Although, in my imagination, I didn't have a brother. That had been a gift beyond measure. I had pictured my parents in my

288

dreams, of course. When Fernando and Christina had said they would adopt me and Carlos, I saw a glimpse of that dream. They weren't exactly the parents of my dreams, but we were going to be one big family. I suppose the word happy should have been inserted in there.

Discovering my real parents were still alive completed my bubble. It had crossed my mind that this would be hard on Fernando and Christina, as they had brought Jose up, but beyond that, I hadn't thought. I'd assumed that Jose, too, would be excited for us to be a real family. Although Jose had his reservations, I'd believed that as soon as he met Leandro and Carolina, there would be an emotional reunion.

I tried not to be judgemental; this was harder for him than it was for me. I figured he needed time, so I would need to be patient.

A shiver swept my spine fearing what the future would bring, and wondering whether I would end up being forced to choose.

The doctor informed me there was an irregularity in the tests, so I was taken to a room and made to lie on a bed where a strange contraption was placed over me. They explained it was taking images of my internal organs. It was both fascinating and frightening at the same time. The images revealed I'd been born with only one kidney; they called it unilateral renal agenesis. Jose and I joked about what a pair we were, with his kidneys being faulty and one of mine missing. Our front helped gloss over the fear we both experienced.

It was decided that I would stay with Fernando and Christina for the time being, as *Mamãe* and *Pai* didn't have their own home and were hiding away in Sebastião's house. Everyone also thought it best if our parents came to visit Jose and me here at the hospital once the sun had gone down and the dark had cast long shadows. They couldn't come to the hotel, and I couldn't visit them at Sebastião's house now that we knew the risk Martinez posed. In the twelve years which had passed, time and hardships had aged them, and the stubble covering the lower half of *Pai's* face was only a casual disguise. If he came face to face with his brother, the recognition would not be tardy in coming.

I still found it hard to reconcile that my nemesis was also my blood uncle.

Martinez swept the streets of Rio like a dredger trawled the riverbed for bodies. Given the physical similarities between me and my parents, it was a struggle to comprehend how he hadn't known who I was all these years. My hatred for him was now more intense than ever. Every bad thing that had befallen my family could be attributed to him. In all my time on the streets, the atrocities I had witnessed, I'd never felt like I do now. Don't get me wrong, if I could have taken the gun that was used to kill DC and Jonny, and turned it on Martinez, I would have. Now, I wanted to make him suffer. My violent thoughts frightened me.

"I'm confused, too, Pedro," Jose replied after I confided my concerns. "I have such conflicting emotions. Whichever way I look at it, I feel like I'm being disloyal."

We lay side by side, something which brought a new poignancy now that *Mamãe* had told us we'd done it as babies. We talked for hours. However much we tried *not* to exclude Carlos, he always seemed to be on the outside.

I think he kept his distance as he knew we had a lot to work through. He came every day to visit with me, with a content look about him, so I guess he was just happy to be off the streets.

Each day *Mamãe* and *Pai* came in, too. *Pai* wore a baseball cap, and *Mamãe* wrapped herself in an elegant headscarf. When Jose said it made her look like a film star, I remembered the time when he had tried to describe a TV to me. Though I now had first-hand experience, I still found the concept confusing. I wanted to know more about how the technology worked. Technology was a word I had picked up from Fernando. I liked to hear him talk since I learnt something new each time.

As the days went by, I could see a thread being stitched whilst we came together as a family. Christina, Fernando, and Carlos left us alone for a while, but I could see how hard it was for them. They must have seen how close we were getting. Christina always acted like a lady, her graciousness and generosity evident despite her world having been turned upside down.

I could see in *Mamãe* the two differing factions which fought in her brain. There was the gentle, beautiful woman who DC had loved, whose love encompassed us all. Yet, some days I would see another woman, one who glared at Christina through narrowed eyes, viewing her as a threat. The pitch of her voice would be higher and she would say strange things. One day she even asked *Pai* when he was going to take her to the hospital to pick up her babies. When he reminded her, with the tenderness one might use toward a young child, that her babies were grown into adolescents now, she had become defensive and told him she knew that, she wasn't stupid. A while later he had held her to him, and I'd got the impression he was stopping her from doing something. The next day she seemed calmer again and asked us about our lives. As much as she showed interest, I could tell that she hated to hear it.

The results finally came through. *Pai* wasn't a match, but *Mamãe* was. *Pai* wasn't pleased. I overheard him admit to Fernando how he feared for his wife's state of mind if she were to go through surgery, when the memories of the past still haunted her present.

The friendship between Fernando and *Pai* grew, each man respected the other. After our alone time as a family, we would all sit together for an hour or so. Fernando and *Pai* talked, both intelligent men, they discussed politics and religion. *Pai* even told Fernando, in detail, about their discovery that had led us to where we are now. I couldn't help wonder how long their new friendship would last, or how strained it would become when the surgery was over and the fight for custody began. It was as though they had agreed to put that battle off until Jose was well again.

Christina and *Mamãe* attempted to get to know each other, but I think their maternal instincts were too strong to bond. Christina feared *Mamãe* would take Jose from her, and *Mamãe* was resentful of the time Christina had spent with her sons.

Carlos, Jose, and I would lie together and talk or play games like Eye Spy, which Jose taught us, but there were only so many things you could see in a hospital room. He also taught us to play cards: Snap, Old Maid, and Gin Rummy.

"Can't we all live together?"

Carlos startled us all with that question. He'd seemed removed from what was going on, but this showed us how much it was affecting him, too. Jose and I both responded with enthusiasm. The adults looked at each other, but no one commented. What his suggestion did was plant a seed.

It also made everyone realise how much we were all affected by this situation.

The Exiles - Brasil

Carolina

Meeting with Pedro was one of the most surreal moments of Carolina's life. Though her mind still pictured him as a baby, she knew he was twelve now. She wasn't stupid; her mind played tricks on her, though. She watched him walking toward her, gangly in the awkward way that boys are when they undergo growth spurts. He wasn't a boy anymore, but neither was he near being a man. Carolina had felt frightened at first, but he knelt in front of her and took her hands, and his words were soothing. She almost asked him if he was a psychiatrist, but then remembered in time that he was a mere child, and he had said he was her son. It was also confusing because there was only one boy, and she knew she'd given birth to two.

Didn't I?

Her remark about knowing Daniel was dead hurt Leandro, she could see it on his face. Carolina didn't feel proud of that, but then, had her husband known his best friend harboured feelings for his wife? She had always known. The puppy eyes he threw her, the eager way he always tried to please her. She'd never encouraged it, but she'd also known he was honourable, and that his allegiance to Leandro superseded any feelings he had for her.

Chapter Seventeen

Jose

Little by little, I got to know Leandro and Carolina. I still thought of them by their first names, but I called them Mum and Dad out loud to appease them. Leandro talked about his previous work when prompted; the passion he felt for it apparent.

"Do you miss it?" I asked.

"Very much, Jose."

"Why don't you do that in England, then? Why do you drive a taxi?"

"When I fled Brasil, I did so on a fake passport. 'Leandro Cordosa' doesn't have a degree or any of the qualifications needed to be a scientist or teach like

Leandro Martinez did. Don't be sad for me, Jose. I am grateful every day that I am alive, and that I have a job which provides for Caro and me. We cannot hanker for the past or what could have been. We have to travel the path that is set before us."

"What did you used to do, Mum?" Carolina sat there in a world of her own; maybe she resided in the past, but I wanted to draw her out.

"I was a pianist, Jose," she said after a short pause.

"Really?" Pedro and I asked together.

"Jinx freeze. Haha."

I had taught him this since we had a habit of saying the same thing at the same time.

"Yes." A smile lit up her face, and in that moment I glimpsed the beautiful woman she'd once been. "I was the best pianist in Rio, maybe the whole of Brasil. Some say I was. When my fingers caressed the keys, I would be transported to another world where only the music and I existed."

"Caro brought tears to even the most hardened person's eyes. I met her when I went to a restaurant where she was playing. She wasn't terribly well-known

298

then. The venue was busy that night, about a hundred and fifty people packed out the little room. I went there because it was renowned for its *Vatapá*, the best in all of Rio. Every Saturday night a pianist would play, but I knew nothing about music. Too studious." He chuckled at the memory. "My table was opposite the piano. I hadn't looked up from my plate of *Vatapá*, the *camarão* were r*equintado* with the *coco*."

I smiled at the expressions crossing his lined face.

"As soon as her fingers stroked the keys, I heard the hauntingly beautiful music. I stopped eating with my fork mid-air, and there it stayed until she stopped. She transfixed me. I could not keep my eyes off her face. Not only was she the most beautiful woman I had ever seen, but there was something in the way she wasn't present in the room. She flew free, like a bird soaring in the calm blue sky. When she came back to the room, her eyes lit upon me and she bestowed me with the gift of her smile. Her eyes danced with mischief while I dripped the juices from my fork down my shirt."

"I came over to help you clean the mark off so that it wouldn't stain your white shirt."

299

Leandro looked up, and in that moment, I felt as though I were a bird who had flown too close to the sun and singed my wings. The look which passed between them must have been what it was like the night when they'd first met. From the things I had seen and heard from Pedro, I guessed that this hadn't happened much, if at all, in the last twelve years.

More than ever my loyalties felt torn. *I* felt torn. Although no one was intentionally doing it, I felt as though both sides had an arm and a leg and were pulling me like a thick-knotted rope in a tug of war.

The doctor entered then, putting an end to the reminiscing.

"*Senhora*, would you come with me so that we can talk through the operation and discuss the risks involved. We need to make sure you are happy to proceed and understand all the risks."

"I'll come with you." Leandro started to rise in his seat.

"No, Leandro, I can do this alone."

The shutters had come down over her eyes masking her emotions. He looked as though he wanted to argue, but she walked up to him and whispered into his ear. The words were not meant for anyone else, but they reached me anyway.

"Say nothing. I can do this one thing for our son. His life is more precious than mine and I will die a thousand deaths if it saves him. Hopefully, it won't come to that." She pressed her lips against his, clasping his face in her hands. His rested on her hips in a gesture more intimate somehow than I could understand. I looked away.

"*Mamãe*." She turned around because she was the only woman in the room. With tears in my eyes and a lump in my throat, I added, "*Eu te amo*," then promptly broke down crying. In less than a heartbeat she had gathered me into her arms and was smothering me with kisses. When she pulled away, I saw that her eyes were as wet as Leandro's, who came to join us. Feeling self-conscious all off a sudden, I pulled back. Seeing a fleeting cloud of sadness in Leandro's eyes, I realised that by pulling back, I had rejected him. He replaced it with a beaming smile before watching with a worried expression. I wanted to make it up to him, but the moment had passed.

The day came that we had all been waiting for. I asked to be alone with Carolina and Leandro for a while before the surgery. I had been on the verge of saying just Carolina, but remembering the hurt expression in Leandro's eyes, I had included him, too. I'd already explained to *Mamãe* and Father why I felt I should, considering the sacrifice that she was making. *Mamãe* had kissed my cheek and said that I didn't have to explain my reasons for wanting to spend time with them.

"You must not feel bad for any feelings you have developed, *Filho*. This is an unusual situation and none of us know how we are supposed to act or feel."

Carolina and Leandro both sat on my bed, like bookends. They both talked and I soon realised that it was as much for their own benefit as it was for mine. Distraction was a great way to avoid thinking about what was happening. After a while, Pedro poked his head around the door and asked to join us.

"Our boys together," Carolina said.

"Our family together," Leandro amended.

Another wave of emotion passed through me causing me to take their hands.

"Group hug?" Pedro asked.

Mamãe and Father found us in the hug when they walked back in.

"They are ready to take you both now to prep you for surgery."

"Please, give me one more minute alone with him?" Carolina asked. "I love you with all my heart. I never stopped loving you."

"*Mamãe*, did you play the piano in England?" I don't know what prompted me to ask that question, but I needed to know.

"No."

"Why?"

"There was no joy in my life when I lost you and Pedro."

Pedro

I couldn't stop the envy from creeping in while I watched Jose bonding with our parents. It was what I wanted, and yet, as I watched them paying more attention to him, I felt betrayed—again. Of course, logically I knew they were spending so much time with him because he was ill, but I discovered that jealousy had no basis in logic. I had called them *Mamãe* and *Pai* from the start, but the deepest emotion elicited was when Jose said *Mamãe*. Twelve years ago, Christina and Fernando had rejected me and taken Jose, and I'd lived with it. Perhaps I was the one best equipped to deal with it, but now it seemed like history was repeating itself as our natural parents gravitated to Jose over me.

At the same time, I despised myself for these thoughts. Jose was my brother, my twin, and I loved him.

I would do anything to protect him. I just didn't know how to handle these emotions. As usual, I painted on a smile and joined in on the family time.

Jose was wheeled out of the room with a worried Christina beside him, holding his hand.

He called out, "Love you, Pedro."

"Love you, too, Jose."

"What is it?"

"Oh, I just want *Mamãe* and you to be safe."

"You know they love us both the same, don't you?"

I shouldn't have been surprised he'd read my mind. "Is nothing sacred?" I joked.

His smile didn't reach his eyes, and tears welled up in mine when I saw again how fragile he looked. The dialysis was taking it out of him.

"I'll walk with you to the operating room."

"No, go to Mum. She needs you."

Mamãe sat in a hospital gown, her long dark hair brushed out and fanning the white garment. *Pai* sat next to her, holding her hand. She stretched out the other hand to me.

305

"I am so glad you came. Sit with me a while."

I sat down without saying a word.

"Pedro, from the moment I held you in my arms I loved you… no, even longer, from when you started to grow inside me. The years apart were unbearable. *Eu te amo, Filho*."

"*Eu te amo, Mamãe*." I threw myself into her arms and sobbed.

"Oh, my little boy, you have had it so tough. I wish I could go back and take the pain for you. You know that I would, don't you?"

Tears choked back my response, so I nodded.

Pai and I walked with her, his arm slung over my shoulder. The ever-present Chad walked with us, like my shadow. We waited in Jose's room; they'd said the surgery would take about four hours. At first we talked, a nonstop barrage of meaningless words, until the words ran dry. Every minute was agony. I kept going over the petty jealousy in my head. What if *something happens?* I needed Jose to know how much I loved him. I even prayed to God—a last resort as I didn't believe in him.

306

Everyone else here did. Well, with the exception of Carlos. He, too, had seen too much to believe in the existence of God, or a benevolent one, as they believed. I was willing to give it a try, to give Him the benefit of the doubt if He existed.

"If you are truly the all-powerful, the all-giving, then show me your power. Bring my *Mamãe* and brother back to me, please."

Carlos came and sat next to me, a silent buttress giving me his support. "They'll be okay, Pedro."

"You think?"

"They've got to be." Desperation was in his voice.

This wasn't just my family, it was his now, too, albeit not blood.

"When have you known anything to go right for us, Carlos? Doesn't all of this seem to be too good to be true?"

Carlos said nothing. We curled up together on Jose's bed, each of us deep in our own thoughts. Fernando stood and paced the floor.

"Sit down, dear," Christina said.

"I can't sit anymore. What is taking so long?"

At that moment the door swung open.

"The operation was a success, both patients are well. They're in the recovery room, and will be a little bit groggy as the anaesthetic wears off. They will both be in a lot of pain. No sharing beds for a while, no overenthusiastic hugs." The doctor looked from me to Carlos as we whooped with joy.

"Boys, be quieter." Fernando grinned, taking the sting out of his words. "We're in a hospital."

Tears flowed mingling with relief as we all hugged. Maybe there was a God after all.

The Exiles – Brasil

Leandro

Leandro watched two of the most important people in his life wheeled away to endure major surgery, which neither of them were equipped for. Jose took after his

Mamãe, Carolina, in many ways. Kind-hearted and gentle, but not made of the stern stuff that Pedro, who resembled Leandro, was. Leandro wanted to protect Jose despite all the advantages he'd had. Maybe it was their circumstances which had shaped them both, but he couldn't help thinking that their personalities had been shaped in the womb.

Leandro had tried to hate Fernando for abandoning Pedro, but couldn't. The man had done what he'd thought was right for his wife, which was something Leandro could relate to. As the days passed, the men found they had shared interests, and that both were of similar intellect and moral code. Though they bonded and formed a friendship of sorts, Leandro knew that when the reckoning came, all that would be forgotten as they fought for their families.

Both boys had been conceived from the love held by Carolina and Leandro. Carolina had nurtured them in her body for nine months and gone through the pain of childbirth, and yet, she'd been denied the right to rear them. It was Fernando and Christina who'd had the pleasure of caring for and teaching Jose how to be a child and grow into a young man. Daniel had done the same for Pedro. In a court of law, whose claim would prove stronger? Who had right on their side morally?

Carlos had mentioned everyone living together as one big family. *Could that work?* Someone had to be in charge. Was it possible for two couples to come to an agreement over the children's future? Fernando and Christina had done everything their way for so long, would they try to assume lead? Jose had turned out well under their care. Leandro considered all the possibilities, pondering whether they could be guided by the other couple. His thoughts strayed to his wife, who lay anaesthetised while her kidney was being removed in order to save their son. Could she cohabit with Christina? Leandro had seen the hateful glances she threw at Christina when she was having an episode, and when she wasn't, she was cordial but no more. He hadn't expected miracles to happen when she reunited with her sons. The truth was, he had never considered anything beyond the actual reunion because a tiny part of him had doubted it would ever happen.

The waiting, which seemed as though it stretched into eternity, was now over. His troubled mind had wandered. The knot in his stomach, and the corresponding nausea, stayed with him long after the doctor declared the operation a success and both patients well, but in need of recovery. The feeling started to fade as he held his wife's hand and saw the smile light her face.

"I did it, Leandro. I gave our son back his life. It was all worth it. My life was worth it."

"What do you mean, *querida*?"

"When we fled Brasil fighting for our lives, I had hopes that we would be reunited with our babies. As the years went by, it didn't seem as though it would happen, and as you know, I couldn't cope. My life seemed pointless, that of a mother without her children, a wife who could not face her duties, a musician without her music. I was only a woman in name, Leandro. Do you understand?"

Leandro nodded although he didn't agree that her life had been pointless. Her life had been brutal, but while hope lay within, anything was possible. They had just proven that.

"Leandro, now I have saved our Jose, I can say that my survival has been validated. My suffering and loss worth it."

"We can start to think about a life with our boys now."

Carolina's smile looked sad. Maybe it was the pain.

"*Eu te amo* with all my heart, Leandro. There was only ever you. Please tell them more about me, about us—the way we were before. Don't let them forget me."

"What are you talking about, Carolina?" Leandro couldn't keep the impatient tone from his voice. It had been a long twelve years, so now her defeatist words were too much.

"*Beije-me , meu querido.*"

Her words erased the frown lines from Leandro's forehead, and a grin spread across his face as he leant over the bed to place his lips on her gentle ones.

"Go now and see our *filho*."

Leandro walked away with a light step. Despite his age and experience, he believed good triumphed against evil, always.

Jose was surrounded by his family. His face was wan; even with medication in his veins Leandro could tell how much he hurt.

"How is Mum?"

"Pretty much the same as you, but she is happy that she could do this for you."

"I want to go and see her," Jose said.

"When you are well enough, but I think she will come to you first." Leandro laughed.

"I want to see her, too," Pedro added.

"She was just going to have a sleep, Pedro. When she is awake and less groggy, she will love to see you."

Excited chatter surrounded the bed but soon Jose looked tired.

"Maybe we should leave you to get some sleep, too." Leandro rose from the chair he had occupied for the last few minutes just as the door opened.

The beaming welcome everyone bestowed on the doctor froze on their faces when they saw the pity in his eyes. His words reached Leandro's ears as he asked to speak to him in private. Leandro didn't need to hear the doctor's words as his legs collapsed under him and the pounding in his chest burst through to his ears.

Chapter Eighteen

Jose

I woke up on a trolley bed in the recuperation room. My thoughts first focused on the waves of sickness that hit me, followed by a severe pain slicing my lower abdomen. In that moment, while my head swam, I felt eyes watching me from the left. Her soft brown eyes were dulled by pain but a smile tugged at the corner of her mouth. Her lips formed the words, "*Eu te amo,*" but no sound came out. I mouthed the words back. I looked at this woman who had given birth to me, and had now given me one of her kidneys, and the power of the bond pulling at me was frightening. Love so overwhelming, such as I had never experienced. I wanted to look away but the pull was too strong. Was feeling this way a betrayal to *Mamãe*? Yet, wasn't this woman my real *mamãe*? Hadn't she been denied the chance to bring Pedro and me up? She had shown her love in so many ways I hadn't considered until now. It tore at a tiny part of me when the porters came and wheeled us both to our separate rooms. Before we parted, she blew me a kiss and winked as though we shared a delicious secret that no one else did.

The memory of those last moments tore at my chest seeing Leandro collapse. I knew that Carolina had died. She had sacrificed herself for me. A scream tore from my lips but the sound wasn't mine. It came from my twin.

"I hate you!" His eyes burned with fury. "You killed her! It's always about you, Jose. Why am I never important?"

Broken, I watched Father gather Pedro's sobbing body and hold my brother tight, calming him. *Is it my fault? Did I kill her? Am I to blame because I was chosen at birth while he had ended up on the streets?* I didn't know.

The doctor strode toward me ordering everyone except *Mamãe* to leave as he started to check me over. "Your blood pressure is high, Jose. You have suffered a terrible loss, but I must insist we keep you calm. I can't stress enough how important it is."

"Was it my fault, *Médico?*" My words trembled. *Mamãe's* fingers curled around my hand.

"No, Jose, your brother is lashing out because he is hurting. People often blame the person closest to them," the doctor answered with a reassuring smile.

Pedro

In the space of a few weeks I'd gone from having everything, to losing it all. I knew it wasn't Jose's fault, he hadn't chosen his life nor had he taken *Mamãe's*, but I couldn't forgive him, illogical as it might be. It wasn't Jose who'd made sure *Mamãe* was happy, looked out for her, reading her moods and doing everything to change them. It wasn't Jose's fault, but he was the favoured child. He was the one everyone thought needed protection, the one who needed to be looked after. For that reason, the result was losing my *mamãe* after such a short time together. For *that,* I couldn't forgive him.

My tears flowed for her, for my loss, but there was also anger mixed in, too, aimed at her. She had made her choice and it hadn't been me. Resentment for Pai also bubbled away inside me. He was so consumed by his own grief that I was not even a secondary factor.

Fernando held me, trying to give me his support, but as he'd been the first person to betray me as a tiny baby, it was hard to accept. Even Christina wasn't blameless; she could have insisted they take me too, should have. Wave after wave of anger and resentment built up until it crashed around me. I pushed away from Fernando and started to run. The sound of his voice as he called my name filtered into my consciousness, but my heart pounded and my feet sped across the polished surface as I ignored him. I dodged the people coming from the other direction, triggering memories of my life of crime.

Even the thought of going back to that didn't slow me down.

The doors opened for me as I ran at them, which was just as well, because I would have barrelled straight into them. My chest, having grown soft over the past few weeks, pulled tight at the exertion. I'd just left the hospital grounds when I realised I stood in the *aléia* where *Pai* and *Mamãe* had been shot after Jose and I were born. I almost expected to see their blood still staining the cobbles. It was strange how this hadn't occurred to me before, but now it symbolised everything that had gone wrong in my life. Rage such as I had never known mushroomed up inside me, and in that moment, I knew the only release would be in the death of Martinez, and I needed to be the one to kill him.

"Pedro?"

A voice which seemed familiar in the vaguest terms stopped me in my tracks. Through clouded eyes, I looked at the man before me who seemed to be showing concern for me.

"My name's Teo. I'm a friend of your *pai*." This man had come into the hospital to deliver a message to *Pai*.

"What are you doing out here? Your *mamãe* and *pai* will be worried about you."

"*Mamãe's* dead." The word's sounded hollow.

His eyes widened and his mouth flew open. I moved to get around him but he grasped my arm, his nails digging into my flesh. "When? How?"

"Just now. A complication from the operation." I doubled up in pain as the words penetrated once more. I would never see her again.

"Come, I'll take you back in."

"I'm not going back in."

Teo said nothing but his hand tightened on my arm. His strength belied his unimpressive frame.

The Exiles – Brasil

Teo

Teo ventured out in the daylight even though he knew the risk involved. He needed to see Leandro. They hadn't met up much since arriving here. Teo knew Leandro had his family now and that one of his boys was ill, but it felt like now that they were back in Brasil, his need for Teo had gone. He'd been resigned to the back shelf, like when they were boys and young men, and Daniel Cortez claimed his attention. Sebastião, too. A stab of jealousy still pierced his chest when he thought of Daniel even though he knew the man was dead and no longer a threat. In England, Leandro had come to Teo. Every day they had met and talked, albeit with the other men, but it might as well have been just the two of them.

When Carolina was in hospital, Teo would call around with a bottle of scotch and they would drink and talk into the night. *"Why do you do it?"* his wife would carp. *"You have eyes for him and he only has eyes for his crazy wife."* Teo knew it to be true. His wife was not a stupid woman. From the first she'd known he could bear no real love for a woman, although he did have a great affection for her. She had wanted a husband, women as plain as her did not attract men. She'd wanted the marital status and Teo had wanted the cover of normality. He did——on the rare occasion——manage to do the dirty deed with her, but in his mind, with his eyes closed, she was Leandro. She knew not to make a sound. In this way they managed to produce three children. Benjy, their eldest, was followed by Helen, and then Marie. Jennifer had insisted that because the babies were born in England, they be given English-sounding names. She'd always believed that one day his tastes would change—if only it were that simple.

Teo never knew if Leandro was aware of his feelings, but he suspected Daniel had known. The way he'd looked at him, the speculative gaze. Daniel probably despised him, but Teo was thankful he'd said nothing.

321

Homosexuality wasn't an accepted part of culture, even if Brasilian Law did not forbid it.

Teo saw Leandro's son as soon as he stepped into the *aléia*. There was so much of Leandro about him. He'd met both boys when he had made an excuse to call in at the hospital. They'd been lying side by side, two peas in a pod. The anger emanating from the boy was powerful. He wasn't like Leandro nor was he like Carolina who, despite her mental illness, was a calm and dignified woman. Teo had never felt pangs of jealousy toward this woman regardless of the all-consuming love Leandro had for her.

"*Mamãe's* dead." His words cut through Teo. He needed to see Leandro, to comfort him. He was aware Pedro was trying to get away, but Teo didn't want the boy running away to be another distraction for Leandro, so he dragged him along in his wake.

Teo was greeted like the conquering hero for bringing Pedro back. Leandro's eyes were misted, red-rimmed, and his face haggard. Teo thought back to when he and Daniel had found him the night he'd been shot and left for dead. He shuddered. Leandro took Pedro from him and held him tight to his chest while they both sobbed.

"Please, *Filho*, don't go again. I can't bear to lose another loved one."

Teo's arms ached to reach out to Leandro, to hold him, and to give him comfort, if only in an innocent gesture.

"First Daniel, and now your *Mamãe*."

Teo staggered backward, the shot hitting home. It had always been Daniel. Never before had Teo felt so angry.

Chapter Nineteen

Jose

It *was* my fault. I knew it, and so did Pedro. It didn't matter what everyone else said. I had taken *Mamãe's* life, my real one, the one who had given me life twice. I had only started to get to know her, was only just learning to love her. Pedro, who had never known a parent's love, had loved her at first sight because he had no internal battle waging. It was simple for him. Carolina was his *mamãe* and Leandro his *pai*. I had taken her from him. Yet again my life had been deemed more important than his. Of course, he hated me.

"It isn't your fault, Jose." Carlos sat on the bed beside me, but I didn't respond. "You couldn't have known she would die. She couldn't cope with life, Jose. This was all she could do for you and she knew it."

I looked at Carlos. "How did you get to be so wise?"

He smiled, a shy lifting of his lips. "Living on the streets, you develop the ability to see beyond the obvious."

We both fell silent; we had no more use for words. Carlos' perceptive qualities did nothing to appease my guilt. It was something I would need to live with.

It was surprising how quickly my body healed. I felt the presence of Mum inside me, which gave me strength and determination. Pedro no longer came to the hospital. Though I yearned for my twin, I understood why he stayed away.

A heavy pall surrounded my room now, the joys of reunion were lost under mourning. A secret funeral ceremony was being arranged by Sebastião. The woman who had set Brasil alight with her music over a decade ago would be interred in secrecy. A plaque with her name on it would be erected once all the players had been rounded up and arrested. Only Leandro and Sebastião would attend. I wanted to be there. After all, she was my mum. Pedro would be fighting to go also, I was sure. Leandro, Fernando, and Christina remained adamant that it was too dangerous.

Leandro's eyes wore an additional layer of pain but his smile was still warm when it lit upon me.

"How is it that you don't hate me?" I asked him when we sat alone.

"This isn't your fault, Jose. Your mum knew what she was doing. It was one of the few things she was certain about. She gave her life for yours, and would have done the same for Pedro had it been required. Pedro is hurting now, but he will see that you are not responsible. He is a sensible young man and he loves you very much. It is time that I go and say my final goodbye to my beautiful wife now."

"Dad, can you say goodbye from me?" I hesitated. "Tell her... I loved her."

Pedro

I stayed cooped up in the hotel which felt like a gilded prison. I couldn't bear to see Jose. My hatred was still directed at him although I knew he wasn't to blame. If I saw him, I knew I wouldn't be able to sustain my anger, though; I wasn't ready to let it abate either.

Watching television proved to be a temporary diversion, as was reading. I longed to go out onto the streets, to make good my promise to kill Martinez. Every bad thing had stemmed from him. Chad or one of the other guards was always with me, though. Which made leaving impossible.

The funeral loomed like a frightening spectre, but I was not allowed to go. "She was my *mamãe*, I have every right to go. You can't stop me. You have no right to tell me what to do."

"Pedro, *meu filho*, it is too dangerous. When this is all over, we will hold a memorial in her name that you and Jose can attend."

"Him!" I spat.

"Pedro, you must not blame your brother. He suffers, too."

"He did not love her. He cared nothing for her."

"That isn't true, Pedro. His loyalties were split." *Pai's* words were soft but held a firm note.

I knew he was right but I wouldn't accept that I couldn't attend my own *mamãe's* funeral. So, I hatched a plan.

The Exiles – Brasil

Teo

Teo no longer cared that he might get caught. The streets of Rio were a salve to his wounds. He knew Leandro

328

would never look at him in *that* way, but that it was always about Daniel cut deep. It hurt. Teo wandered the streets without worrying where he was going.

"*Desculpa.*" his words rushed out as he walked into an unmoving barrier of the human kind.

His eyes dilated as he saw first the uniform, and then the man inside it. Sweat formed on his brow and in the palms of his hands. Teo looked away and tried to make his escape before the spark in Martinez's eyes became recognition.

"*Esperar!*" the *policial* barked.

Teo waited, his heart beating faster than normal, so loud that he feared Martinez would hear it.

"I know you?"

He sighed. The penny hadn't dropped yet. "No, Detective Inspector. I am new to this area."

"Your papers. I want to see them."

"I don't carry them, Detective Inspector. I can bring them down to the station."

Martinez started to nod, but then his eyes widened. "Teo..?" he whispered, almost unsure, but then the dawning recognition in his eyes was complete.

Teo considered running but knew Martinez's man would catch him in no time. Within moments Teo's arms had been pulled behind him and handcuffed, and then he was bundled into the back of the *polícia* van. The back of the van smelt of urine and vomit. Teo shuddered at the thought of what would happen to him when they arrived at the *polícia* station. He had no grand illusions as to the treatment of prisoners here. It wasn't like England, which had become his second home. There was no small amount of irony in the fact he'd hated England, the cold, the people who seemed to lack emotion and were as frigid as the air they breathed. He had longed for his homeland, the feel, the warmth on his skin, the colourful, passionate people whose voices rumbled in the air, and yet, he had been safe in England. On the whole the *polícia* were trustworthy, unlike in his beloved Brasil, where justice was a thing that could be bought or sold, and had nothing to do with right or wrong.

He lost all sense of time while lying there. The van twisted and turned so much Teo couldn't follow which direction they were going, but his body swayed with the movements. Tears formed in the corners of his eyes which he blinked back. Tears were a sign of weakness, and weakness could be exploited. The vehicle ground to a halt making Teo fall flat of his face; blood trickled from his nose on impact. His arms were cuffed and in the air. As much as he would have liked to have been in a position to react, he lay like a fish out of water, unable to move.

A heavy clunk indicated the catch on the van's doors opening. Rough hands grabbed his forearms and dragged him out before throwing him to the ground. Teo spat out a mixture of mud and blood. Instinct told him to use his hands to wipe the mess, but they were trussed up behind him. He looked up, blinking under the glare of the sun after the dark enclosed space.

A quick scan of the area made him aware that they were not at the *polícia* station. This was scrubland outside the city perimeters. *If he can kill his own brother in cold blood, why would he hesitate to kill me?* Bile rose in his throat.

"You have nothing to fear, Teo. I would not shoot a man who is defenceless. Your cuffed hands tell the world you are harmless."

Teo's heart slowed down. *Maybe he only wants to talk.*

"Uncuff him," Martinez ordered the officer beside him.

Teo inhaled and exhaled. Freedom was within his grasp.

"However, a man who wears no cuffs could have been trying to attack me."

Teo's eyes popped. "No, wait! Don't shoot." The gun was already levelled at his face. In that split second his anger and the belief that he'd been betrayed by Leandro resurfaced. "I have information you want."

Martinez's hand wavered but he kept his aim true.

"I will trade it for my life." Teo's words trembled in unison with his body.

Martinez's maniacal laughter echoed around them. "Every man has his price."

In that moment Teo hated himself as much as he hated Martinez.

"If the information is of no interest to me?"

"It will be."

Martinez's finger hovered a millimetre from the trigger. Teo felt warm wetness spread through his trousers and trickle down his legs. His shame was met by mocking laughter from both officers.

For a brief second, Teo considered telling Martinez to go to hell, but then Daniel's face popped up to taunt him and he blurted out, "Leandro is still alive. He and Carolina did not die when you shot them."

The rage erupting from Martinez made Teo quail. His colouring turned a purplish red as he screamed, "*Bastarda, bastarda!*" After a moment he stopped and turned his cold eyes back to Teo. "How do I know you are not lying?"

"He will be at the *cemitério* today at five pm. Carolina died giving one of their sons a kidney. He will be there. I believe you know one of them? Pedro, he lived on the streets."

Martinez's brows drew together and his jawline tightened. "I knew there was something about that boy."

Teo had been on the verge of telling him about the investigation, too, when Martinez's arm rose, steadying on his target. His finger moved a mere fraction.

"You promised."

"I lied."

The rapport of the gunshot sounded in the silence while its impact threw Teo backwards. After that, there was nothing.

Chapter Twenty

Jose

I was sitting up in bed when the door swung open. "Pedro?"

"Jose, we have to talk. Where is everyone?"

"*Mamãe* and Father have taken Carlos out to get some food. They're bringing it back here. Father was then going to see you. He didn't want you to be alone today."

I acknowledged Chad with a slight inclination of my head, and he nodded back then took up his station by the wall.

"We need to talk in private. Can you make an excuse of going to the bathroom? Suggest I accompany you," Pedro leaned in and whispered.

I did as he asked.

"I'll come with you, too," Chad said.

"Will you wait outside, then? Not being funny, Chad, but a boy doesn't need a full audience. Pedro will be there with me as it is."

"Okay, but you holler if you need me."

I couldn't walk fast; the *médico* had suggested gentle exercise but also warned me not to overdo it. I figured this wasn't overdoing it.

The door to the toilet closed and Pedro threw some of my clothes at me from a rucksack. "Quick, change."

"What?"

"We're going to *Mamãe's* funeral. They can't stop us."

"But they won't let us leave."

"That window is low enough for us to climb out."

"We're on the fourth floor," I gasped.

"There's a rail outside, with steps leading down. The emergency exit is right next to the toilets. Hurry." The urgency in his voice convinced me.

"I know it wasn't your fault—"

I stopped him. "You don't have to say anything, Pedro. I know."

His head leaned against mine for a brief second before he bent down and put my shoes on for me. Even though the ledge was low, my stitches pulled as I climbed. I didn't tell Pedro. The walkway was positioned about four inches from the side of the building. It was hard, but I tried not to wince at the pain that erupted when I stretched.

"Are you alright?" Pedro hissed.

"Yes."

"Quiet then, while you walk down the steps."

We reached the bottom without incident, although it had taken me longer than expected. Pedro couldn't contain his impatience.

"Taxi."

"We have no money, Pedro, and I can't run."

"I have money."

"You do? How?"

"I found it."

"Found it? Where? In Father's wallet?"

"Ask me no questions, I'll tell you no lies."

We slid into the back of a taxi just as Chad came racing out of the hospital.

"*Cemitério*, driver," Pedro ordered.

Chad caught sight of us.

"They'll be worried about us."

"We'll be back soon enough. We should be there."

The car crawled through the streets, the driver had no sense that we had to be somewhere soon.

"Drive faster please, sir," Pedro urged.

"You running from someone, boys?"

"No. Our *mamãe* is being buried. *Pai* thought we were too young to go, but we have to. You understand?"

His eyes viewed us in the rear view mirror. Nodding, he changed up a gear and the car picked up pace. We pulled up at the *cemitério* in time to see Leandro and Sebastião standing beside a freshly dug grave. Sebastião's hand rested on Leandro's shoulder. A priest walked over looking furtive and ill at ease.

Pedro

Dipping Fernando's wallet was child's play, but I did feel guilt. In spite of everything he knew about me, he trusted me enough to leave his valuables lying around. I suppose he thought I no longer had a reason to steal since food came to me for free. Normally he would have been correct, but I needed the money right now as much as I'd once needed food.

It was also easy talking Chad into taking me to the hospital. *"I have been unfair to Jose, Chad. It isn't his fault and I want him to know it today. He shouldn't be alone. I know Christina and Carlos will be there, but we have a special bond and he needs me—and I need him."* That fixed it, as I'd known it would. Chad expected danger around every corner, except from us kids. Looking at his huge muscles and the gun strapped to his chest, I pitied anyone who crossed him. I hoped he wouldn't get into too much trouble from Fernando.

Seeing Jose sitting up in the hospital bed made me realise how I had taken for granted that he would recover. A shiver travelled my spine realising I could have lost him too, and that my last words to him would have been cruel and senseless.

I hatched a plan where we could escape Chad, using a trip to the bathroom as an excuse. The pain was etched over Jose's face when he started to climb, but I needed us to go. I knew that he, like me, would regret it for life if we didn't, so I chose to pretend I hadn't seen each wince, that I didn't feel his physical pain as though it were mine. I hadn't told anyone how I'd experienced pain during Jose's operation because I hadn't wanted anyone to worry.

We pulled up outside the *cemitério* as the priest turned up. There would be no church service, this had to be low key. After paying the driver, Jose and I stepped from the taxi. Now that we were here, it felt daunting. It was one thing to be brave and assertive in the safety of one's home, but being faced with the reality of the situation was another thing altogether.

Jose's hand slipped into mine and squeezed. I didn't need to look at him to know he knew what I was feeling, but I did glance at him. A tear formed in the corner of his eye. He didn't attempt to wipe it away, and for that, I considered him brave.

Pai's face showed mixed emotions when we walked up to the grave, anger and pride at the same time. We had broken the rules, yes, but it was proof of our love. After a sharp rebuke he hugged us both close.

The ceremony was short while the priest kept looking around him, fearful of the consequences, no doubt. His words meant nothing to me until he said *Mamãe's* name. It was clear he hadn't known her, but *Pai* had told him about her life, which he described in brief. Four men arrived, each taking one of the straps that lay beneath the casket. With a solemn air, they lifted the straps and then lowered *Mamãe* into the ground.

Tears flowed from my eyes, stinging as they slid over my cheeks. I wanted to scream out loud but a hand squeezed mine. I didn't need to look at Jose to know his face reflected mine. I gripped his hand, curling my fingers around his.

Pai stood behind us and placed a hand on our shoulders, then scooped us both into a hug. We heard cars pull up. Fernando and Chad walked across the *cemitério* with a respectful pace although both were probably seething.

"Boys. You've had us all worried. M– Christina is beside herself," Fernando said.

His word choice earned Fernando the utmost respect from me when he chose not to dishonour my *mamãe* at her funeral by naming the woman who had borne the title that she should have.

The tranquillity of the *cemitério* was broken by the crunch of determined feet.

"Paolo."

"Martinez."

Pai and I spoke together, our words trembling.

"I will kill you!" I screamed and rushed at Martinez before anyone could stop me. His laugh was demonic and mocking as he lifted up his gun. I stopped.

"So, Pedro, you were my nephew all along. Scum like you belong on the street. Had I known who you were, I would have made sure you were killed along with your friend Jonny and that pervert DC."

"Take that back!" I shouted.

"DC was Daniel Cortez." *Pai* stepped forward.

A vein jumped out on the side of Martinez's face at this information.

"Brother, I heard you lived. Your lover boy Teo could not wait to give you up in exchange for his pathetic life."

Leandro gasped. "And you killed him anyway?"

A smile curled up the corners of Martinez's lips. I found him smiling scarier than when he wore his usual scowl.

"You will die this time. You escaped death twice at my hands. You should have died all those years ago with *Mamãe* and *Pai,* but now you will all die, starting with you, little nephew."

My heart stopped as his gun centred on my chest. I saw Chad out of the corner of my eye raise his gun but he was too late to stop the bullet. Frozen to the spot, in my peripheral vision someone else moved, followed by two more gunshots. I was still standing, but Fernando lay bleeding at my feet because he'd intercepted the bullet meant for me with his own body. Martinez and the other officer were hit by clean shots from Chad's gun. All around me, screams and frantic activity broke out as everyone rushed to help Fernando.

I stayed where I was, unable to move, mute. All my brain could comprehend was that Fernando had put me first, and I had let him down. If I hadn't talked Jose into coming, he would still be alive.

The Exiles – Brasil

Leandro

Jose and Pedro walked toward Leandro as he stood at the *cemitério*. His heart was so full of pride he thought it would burst. Though danger was inherent, his boys had braved it all to say goodbye to his Carolina. He knew if she could see them, she would have been happy. A state which had eluded her for too many years. Leandro knew he would need to get Jose back to the hospital straight after, the boy looked pale and uncomfortable, but he would not turn them away now.

Silent tears marched like soldiers down his face. The boys both cried for the *mamãe* they had got to know too late. Leandro wrapped his arms around them to give comfort, but to also satisfy the craving for comfort he had as well. He'd longed to hold his sons for so many years now. Leandro had buried his own feelings in order to support Carolina, whose pain was worse than his, having carried them for nine months.

It was inevitable that Fernando and the bodyguard would turn up to look for the boys. It was, after all, what a good father did. He looked out for his sons. Pedro was just relating how they had eluded Chad which made him want to chuckle. Carolina would have loved that in the early days. During her pregnancy they'd discussed what they thought their child would be like; they had only thought in the singular. Both agreed that a little spark of independent spirit would suit them well, as long as they were respectful and studious.

Pedro and Leandro saw Martinez at the same time. Leandro wanted to run, to grab his family and get them to safety, but there was no time. He watched, helpless while Fernando took a bullet for his son. Leandro, still reeling from finding out Teo had been killed, was taking a moment to register that Paolo had just admitted to also killing their parents. They'd both been killed in a house fire that had been considered accidental. Leandro had climbed out through a window moments before their home had collapsed amidst licking flames and clouds of dust.

Pedro rushed at Martinez, who raised the gun. Leandro reached out to pull him back but encountered air instead. Fernando's reactions were swifter. Leandro watched as his new friend's body was thrown backward as a bullet ripped through him. More shots rang out and Leandro's brother hit the deck, followed by the officer with him.

Sebastião reached Fernando to give him aid, but the shot had gone straight though his heart. Leandro pulled

Jose away from the blank, unseeing eyes staring up at them. He held the boy's thrashing body against him, stroking his hair to soothe him, knowing that they were only feeble gestures to a boy who'd just seen his father killed. Pedro stood stock still; he hadn't moved or uttered a word. Reaching out with his free hand, Leandro tried to pull him in close, but he reacted as though he'd been burnt.

"I'm so sorry, Jose. It's all my fault. If I hadn't insisted we come, Fernando would still be alive."

Leandro acknowledged to himself the truth behind these words, although he knew his son wasn't to blame. If he had not come, Leandro realised, he himself would have died, and so would've Sebastião, as there wouldn't have been an armed guard there to stop Paolo.

Epilogue–Sixteen years later

Jose

I would like to say that we lived happily ever after, that life was easy and the challenges we faced were few. I'd like to, but I can't.

Watching my father get shot down in front of me was the single most harrowing experience of my life. My brother blamed himself and was withdrawn for months. I tried not to agree with him, but part of me couldn't help but concur with him. That was then, though; this is now, and somehow we managed to come out the other end as rather decent chaps.

Mamãe was devastated at the loss of her husband, but from somewhere she drew on reserves even she hadn't known she had. She and Leandro talked long and hard in those first few weeks, the outcome of which was that they decided to pool their resources for joint custody of Pedro, Carlos, and me. *Mamãe* was adamant that we return to England, at least initially.

"We can regroup there in the knowledge that we are safe."

It took a while to sort out the correct documentation for Leandro, Pedro, and Carlos, but with a few strings pulled and favours called in, we were able to set off back to my home.

It was inevitable, I suppose, that after a few years of mutual appreciation and respect, love grew between *Mamãe* and Leandro. Some would call it a neatening off of loose ties. I was an awkward, spotty fifteen-year-old at the time, with raging hormones, and the idea that *Mamãe* was still capable of those kind of feelings at her age—not that she was old or anything—made me feel ill. *"It makes me wanna vomit,"* was the unfortunate phrase I often used.

Carlos blossomed in England, where fear no longer creased his brow. He became a young man with a quiet, assured confidence. We stayed in England until he had finished sixth form, and then we returned to Brasil, where he enrolled in university. It was his drive and passion which shaped all of our lives as we followed his dream.

Pędro

"Pedro, I know what I want to do." The boy's young eager eyes looked up at me, waiting for my approval, as he did every week when he came up with a new idea.

"So, Raoul, what do you want to do?" I could have added 'this week' but discouraging dreams was not part of my remit or my personality.

"I want to work here. I want to be a psychologist like you."

I smiled. The light shining from his eyes burned brighter than I had ever seen them, and this time I believed he had found his calling.

"Okay, Raoul. Have you spoken to Carlos about this? Found out what qualifications you need? The subjects you need to focus on?"

His head hung low and his eyelids drooped.

"Raoul, I think you could be great in this role, but you need to apply yourself academically first, and we need to work on that self-confidence more."

He looked at me with a spark of hope. "You think I could do it? A boy from the streets."

"Look at me and Carlos, and everyone else who works here."

"Except Jose."

"*Si*, except Jose."

"And Christina."

"*Mm-hmm, si* Leandro also," I added with a little laugh since I knew where he was going with this.

We had set up the centre ten years ago. It had started as a shelter for homeless waifs and strays with pallet beds in a long dormitory, and a place where we provided food and clothing. We'd bought out an old dilapidated factory. At first, we had contented ourselves by providing the safe environment described, even though our plans, or should I say Carlos' plans, were on a much more epic scale. From the time he had first mentioned his dream, which was a continuation of his parents' lifelong wishes, I had known what I wanted to do. It became a family venture. *Pai* received compensation for the trauma and years of exile. Christina sold her home in England, Fernando's business, and some shares he'd had in various different concerns. *"We should keep some to provide an income for us to live off,"* Christina had said.

Jose ran the centre; his skills in administration and ability to negotiate were second to none. His attention to detail ensured we always had what we needed. Carlos became a careers advisor after we ventured out beyond just providing a safe space. We wanted to take these children and help them create a life for themselves. I trained as a psychologist, and then listened to their horror stories, allowing them release in a safe environment. This had been a natural progression for me after my life on the streets and the personal trauma I had lived through while I blamed myself for Fernando's death. *Pai* took me to see a psychiatrist in England who *Mamãe* had seen, and he helped me find perspective along with a passion for the human mind and how to help heal it.

Christina helped wherever she was needed. Her niche became being a much needed and loved mother figure—a role for which she was cut out. *Pai* retrained as a primary school teacher. Our children couldn't be placed straight into the state system, so he taught them at whatever level they needed until they were ready to enter school. For one young man, he also gave additional support to guide him through university. We didn't have the resources to take every child off the street, but we were able to set up a drop-in food kitchen which was open to everyone. We had a waiting list for children to join the centre. Our capacity was for fifty live-in residents.

Each month we—the board, which was made up of the founders—met and discussed strategy and how we could move forward. Our latest plans were to open a second centre, and Jose was tasked with finding the right location and building. He had also managed to secure a small amount of government funding along with additional funding from a few of the bigger local businesses. He was in the process of approaching international companies to see what could be attained. Carlos was pushing for practical workshops, hands on work—engineering, mechanics, carpentry, and more. We all loved the idea, but the funding required would be phenomenal.

"It could pay for itself over time, especially a garage. We get trained mechanics and bring in real work, which pays while those boys who are interested get on-the job training."

"It would be great for their confidence," I averred.

Jose wrote it down. *"Maybe we could start by getting these boys apprenticeships in existing garages to see how it pans out while I figure out how to get the funding?"* We all agreed that this was a suitable and temporary compromise.

"Pedro. Pedro?"

I looked up. "Sorry, Raoul. I was lost in thought. Come on, let's go talk to Carlos and Leandro to see what extra support they can provide for you." Raoul threw his arms around my neck and squeezed so tight I thought he was going to choke me. "Okay, enough, Raoul."

He ran to the door pulling it open for me. "Pedro, Mrs Martinez is here." He blushed, as did all the boys, when he looked on the angelic face of my wife.

"Raoul, I'll meet you in Carlos' office in a few minutes. Ask him to wait until I arrive."

"*Si*, Pedro. Mrs Martinez." He smiled, a cheeky dimple appearing as he bounded away.

Alea stepped inside my room and closed the door, then reached up on tip toes to plant a kiss on my lips. My hands splayed around her stomach, cupping our twins.

"How are the boys behaving today?"

"The girls have been great," she asserted with a chuckle.

"*Pai* just had a meeting with an Italian woman, Analise, who is interested in doing charitable work. Her Papa is said to be one of the richest men in Italy and he indulges Analise by giving her anything she wants. I suggested she meet with Jose."

"Maybe we could all meet her?'

"Not so fast, handsome. Jose can handle it—and I think she might be his type, if you know what I mean." I knew what she meant, and I hoped she was right. I wanted Jose to find as much happiness
as I had.

The Exiles – Brasil

Leandro

"Do you want dinner out tonight, Christina?"

"*Hmm*?" She pushed the glasses up from her nose and sat them atop her hair which was only just starting to show a peppering of grey. The newspaper she discarded onto the coffee table. "What was that, my love?"

"Just wondering if you wanted to eat out tonight?"

"It's not a special occasion, is it?"

"No, I just wanted to spoil my beautiful wife."

"Did you ever think we could be this happy, Leandro?"

"You mean after the tragedies we suffered?"

"Yes."

"We deserve to be. When Carolina died, I thought I could never be happy again, but I had the boys to pull me through. Then you lost Fernando and your world imploded, but you, too, found strength in our boys. Your courage and beauty touched me to the core. When we first got together, we were two lost souls seeking solace."

"And now?"

"Are you fishing, my darling?" Her soft laugh pulled at Leandro's heartstrings. "I cannot lie. I have been happier these years with you than I ever imagined, even after the troubles we've had. I could not wish the deaths of our loved ones to have achieved this bliss, though. You understand?" he asked.

She nodded and leant across to place her lips on his.

"Have you met this Analise yet?" she asked.

"Yes, Jose is smitten, and she seems to be, too. She has promised that her papa will fund the new centre and a few of the workshops."

"Well, I think it's about time he brought her around to meet his *mamãe*." She sniffed, pretending to be annoyed.

The phone interrupted them. Leandro rose to pick it up. He whooped out loud.

"Granny, grab your bag we're going to the hospital."

Christina squealed. "Alea has had the babies? What are they? Is she okay?"

"Sebastião says *Mamãe* and her boy and girl are all fine."

Christina wrapped her arms around his neck. "Come on, Grandpa. We can't let Grandpa Sebastião have them all to himself." She paused. "Now, all we need is for Carlos to find someone."

"Carlos has the centre. That is all he wants."

"We'll see."

Leandro chuckled before lacing his fingers with his wife's and leading her to the car to meet their grandchildren.

The End

Glossary Brasilian to English:

Aléia	Alley
Ambulância	Ambulance
Avô	Grandad
Bastarda	Bastard
Bebê	Baby
Beije-me , meu querido	Kiss me, my darling
Bom Dia	Good Morning
Brigadeiros	Chocolate Truffles
Burro Burro	Dumb arse
Camarão	Shrimp
Cemitério	Cemetary
Coco	Coconut
Coração	Heart
Desculpa	Sorry
Deus	God
Dinheiro	Money
Esperar	Wait
Eu te amo	I love you
Favelas	Shanty Town
Feijoada	Black bean & Meat Stew
Filho	Son
Lago	Lake
Mamãe	Mum

Requintado	Exquisite
Médico	Doctor
Meu bebê	My Baby
Minha Querida	My Darling
Moqueca	Stew (Fish)
Não	No
Olá	Hello
Pai	Father
Pivetinho	Street Child (slang)
Polícia	Police
Policial	Police Officer
Político	Politician
Prostituta	Prostitute
Saúde	Cheers
Senhor	Sir
Sim	Yes

Vatapá A Brazilian dish made from bread, shrimp, coconut milk, finely ground peanuts and palm oil mashed into a creamy paste.

About the Author

 Self-published author bursting with enthusiasm and ideas that can't be contained in my head so spill out onto paper. I predominantly write romance but I am playing with other genres.

I have enjoyed reading and writing from a tender age, and I realised recently that the magic of childhood that we lose as an adult can be found again if we open our eyes to the beauty all around us. I find inspiration in so many different situations and have approximately thirty something WIPs. A Boy from the Streets came about when I was researching for one of my other books. I bought Christina Lamb's book "Small Wars Permitting: Dispatches from Foreign Lands" I was looking for some information on being a foreign correspondent. I was horrified by what I read within those pages about the street children in Brazil but it did give me an idea for this book and the words flowed.

Thank you for reading A Boy from the Streets. If you enjoyed this book, please consider dropping by Amazon or Goodreads to leave me a review.

Also if you would like to connect with me you can do so by visiting my website, Facebook or Twitter pages:

Website:
https://gibbsdream.wordpress.com/

Facebook: http://on.fb.me/1Iu9LuY

Twitter: https://twitter.com/gibbsdream

More by this Author

As Dreams are Made on (Novelette)

Newly wed Matty Taylor is plagued by visions that force her to seek out a Gypsy at a local fair. Dragged violently into a frightening dream world, she is soon rescued by the mysterious Thomas Trevelyan and taken to his secluded house in the woods.

Will her husband, Donald, suspend his disbelief and wake her from her nightmare?

Can Thomas win her heart and keep her from the lure of her real life and the love of her husband?

A Lifetime or a Season (Novelette)

Athena finds herself in the wet and windy South Coast of England as she tries to forget the enigmatic man who ignited her dreams.

Roberto seems determined to hold her at arm's length but can't seem to set her free once and for all.

Having lived in the shadows of her self-centred mother, Athena struggles to find her true identity.

A Lifetime or a Season is a journey of personal discovery for Athena as she takes an independent step into the unknown in order to achieve a life-long dream.

Will she find the love that she is searching for with Roberto or will the sacrifice be too much?

The Storm Creature (Novelette)

At eighteen, Lucy had everything going for her: a supportive family, a rapt audience, and her dream of becoming a published author about to be realised.

A single moment in time on a dark, rainy road changes things forever.

That was then, but this is now. Lucy has suffered through eight years of haunting visions and thoughts with every raging storm thanks to a tempestuous storm creature who torments her. What does the baleful creature want with Lucy? Will the troubled woman ever be able to let go of the past and forgive herself?

Or will she sacrifice everything she holds dear?

Recommended Indie Author

Rose English

Hope is all Emmeline has.

Under rolling storm clouds and raging thunder, the Gods unleash their wrath upon the earth, and in the chaos of the countryside awash with rivulets, Alfie Beeson is felled by some unseen force. With a desperate burst of strength, Emmeline drags her unconscious husband back to their cottage.

Throughout the winter she ministers to his needs, following her Grandmother Aspasia's recipes collected over the years in her delicately penned 'Home Remedies'. Alfie appears to be on the mend when the gentle, shivering snowdrops begin to raise their dainty heads above the snow, bringing hope. However, as the little flowers creep from the forest up to the cottage, Alfie takes a turn for the worse. By the time the blooms are close enough to tap upon the door, she has lost her love. Grieving and bereft, Emmeline tries to cope without her soulmate. Her broken heart causes even her gentle artwork to suffer. Paintings are left unfinished in the parlour.

With the arrival of The Anniversary comes a surprise visitor. Will this visitor rekindle the light in Emmeline's delicate brown eyes?

Can the hole in her heart ever be healed?

This heartfelt short story now includes a sample of some of Aspasia Cherry's A~Z of Herbal Remedies along with poetry, a few myths and a little magic about the local flora that would have been found in and around Emmeline's cottage.

Website: https://roseenglishukauthor.wordpress.com/

Amazon link: http://amzn.to/2iBjtZC

Printed in Great Britain
by Amazon